Father, Creator, Spirit –

Surrender

by

Deborah Lamoreaux

Fascinated, he watched as the very last of her life drained right out of her eyes and slender form. Just slipped away, ever so silent, as though it had never existed.

As though she had never existed.

One more down. Only limitless millions to go.

There was just something so intriguing about the way some souls left the earth. It appealed to him on a visceral level. Bringing out the predator in him he supposed. It was like he could almost taste that special, very best part of them, so true and so pure, moving through their fragile, puerile, and pathetic static bodies for the very last time. Leaping, pulsing with joy at the knowledge of what was to come…at last.

And then there were the others–the ones who went to the void. He'd journeyed there many times himself, to the place where prayers are no longer answered. Or heard. And those who suffered there eternally moved their lips, formed the words, tried to scream, but were denied even that release–their bone-dry throats emitting no sound.

Ever.

And still they scurried around, so many of them. Clammy, ice-cold fingers grasping in the darkness. Traveling up and down, floors upon floors of a virtual maze of snares and perpetual torment. Unending and inescapable levels of despair.

So busy doing nothing, the damned.

Nothing that would ever matter, ever again. Nothing that could change the inevitable conclusion– the most horrific of fates.

There were countless of his kind in the strange, nightmarish realm. But he didn't want to belong there. In truth, he doubted he belonged anywhere.

Strange, but a human had stopped and prayed for him once, long ago, in his time of despair. Out of nowhere he appeared, looked deep into his eyes as he wrapped a hand of comfort around his clenched fist. He'd allowed himself to hold on for just a second and there had been such warmth, such peace in that instant. What a glorious glimpse of salvation in that mere touch. A farce though. For redemption was something he knew he could never have.

He shrugged off the memory, for be it Purgatory or eternal damnation, it was all the same to him. For him, there'd be no joyful welcome.

Only another brand of unceasing torment.

Like a lover who'd just lost his beloved, he touched her face one last time. Even as he savored the last ripples of sensation, like a predator reliving a chase. Lifting her silky blond head from his lap, he let it drop. Felt nothing, at the sight of her body, stretched out upon the cold, hard floor.

Instead, he sighed in disappointment that once again he'd missed the mark, as slowly he rose, transforming by degrees, inch by agonizing inch, back into the one he despised.

On swift feet, he exited the room and disappeared, into the darkness.

Chapter 1

1Thessalonians 5:17-18
Pray without ceasing.
In everything give thanks: for this is the will of God in
Christ Jesus concerning you…

Rissa sensed the change in her surroundings. She was in that place again…between sleep and waking…

But something was different this time… felt different this time.

Her anxiety grew as she acknowledged this was no dream. This 'travelling' she did while she was asleep, was real after all.

Where was she now?

She opened her eyes a crack and looked around. She was hovering in mid-air, in what looked like a huge, very noisy stadium, filled to the gills with thousands of beings. Blurry, like looking through a dirty, unfocused lens, try as she might, she just couldn't see them clearly and the not knowing only heightened her fear.

As she sometimes did in these strange circumstances when she was afraid, she closed her eyes again and began humming her favorite hymn–under her breath at first, and then singing loudly, as if she could somehow drown out the din of garbled chatter around her as she hoped for strength to endure, until she could escape, or wake from this, her latest trial.

And the most miraculous thing happened–a voice began to sing with her. At first just a few joined her choir of one, and then more and more, until the swell of voices singing praises to God, resonated all around her.

WHAM!

Her eyes snapped open as she was jarred to the bone by a sudden blast of icy energy, accompanied by the most menacing roar she'd ever heard in her life. The force of it filled the space around and beneath her, bumped her up a few feet and then just as quick, dropped her down again.

Pure, unadulterated rage surrounded her now, like a living presence.

And fear.

As the ones who had just joined in singing

praises to her King scurried away in all directions. Trying to hide themselves from the wrath of evil.

Someone, or something, grasped her hand then, yanking her away, pulling her through the air at mind-numbing speed. Looking at the chaos she left in her wake, heartbeat pounding in her ears, she could see the far-off darkness expand like a living being, closing in, devouring everyone and everything in its path.

Coming for her.

Faster…faster please!

In her mind she willed her rescuer to propel them along at an even more swift pace.

On her back, with her arm stretched out behind her, she had a front row view of the approaching evil, but try as she might, she couldn't even turn her head to the side to catch a glimpse of the one who held her hand in such a tight and reassuring grip.

In a flash she was flung forward. Out of the dark tunnel she tumbled, out onto the ground and into the open air. Utterly alone, she stood up and took a moment to look around. The tunnel was gone and thankfully so were its inhabitants and the encroaching darkness.

She was standing on the bank of a river.

How bizarre…

In shock, the residual fear and despair closed in on her and as she hung her head trying to catch her breath, she fought the sudden swell of tears that threatened to overwhelm her.

Don't you cry. Crying never solves anything.

A voice from her past echoed in her mind, even as a dozen thoughts and questions struggled for precedence.

Why was this happening? What had she done wrong? Why her? What should she do?

Trembling, she felt her composure about to slip away, she inhaled deeply as she lifted her head and there he was.

A man.

Waving.

Across the water, standing on the bank, on the opposite side.

About her age, he was average height, had wavy black hair and the most welcoming smile she'd ever seen.

And holding…

Was that a cardboard sign?

She'd only ever seen one once, in a museum.

And on it, in big black letters.

Just one word–

PRAY

Seriously?

He nodded and pointed to his recommendation and grinned, as though he could read her thoughts and was there to provide a timely response to her most perplexing questions.

You've got to be kidding me.

She forgot her predicament for the moment.

Singing hymns was easy in this dream-like realm she'd discovered, but talking was hard. No matter how she tried, many times she just couldn't give voice to words that seemed to only echo in her mind.

Worse yet, for her, the garbled sounds emitted by those poor souls she'd encountered, with the frantic hands, grasping for her in the darkness, were nothing but gibberish.

Dead men tell no tales...

Nevertheless, she took a deep breath and prepared to call out.

Gasping as she was jolted awake, Rissa sat up in bed.

"What in the world?"

Wide awake now, she placed a shaky hand to her chest, where her heart still beat out a rapid rhythm, wondering what had awakened her, just as she was about to–

BAM! BAM!

She jumped again as the sound of someone knocking on her front door scared the wits out of her. Rising, she reached for the dressing gown hanging over the back of her rocking chair and shrugged it on.

BAM! BAM! BAM! The knocking came again.

This time more insistent and louder, propelling her on swift, bare feet out of her bedroom, past the kitchen and into the living room.

"Coming, coming!" she yelled on her way to the door, to forestall a third round of banging she felt sure would result in damage to some part of the prized and very rare brass knocker she'd just managed to find, to match her antique door.

"Yes, what is it?!" Her tone sounded sharp to her ears as she yanked it open only then realizing that in her haste and anger, she'd neglected to first look through the peephole.

"Good morning, ma'am, I'm detective superintendent Duncan Wright from the 15th precinct." Her offending visitor briefly held up a badge. "We've had a recent suspicious death of a woman in the area." He removed his shades. His squinting gaze skimmed her from the top of her head to her bare toes and then back up again.

"I can see I woke you–" he glanced at his watch and gave her a disapproving look.

She felt her simmering anger build.

Is he seriously judging me right now?

"–but would you mind if I came in to ask you a few questions?"

"Yes, I would mind, actually." Her response was clipped and dripping with as much ice as she could gather.

His left brow made a swift climb, almost to his

hairline.

"Ma'am–?"

There was just something about the way he said that word. Grr! She clenched her jaw. It should have been a means of showing respect to the listener, but instead it sounded like an insult to her 32-year-old, single ears, making her just want to smack him!

"–I just need a few minutes of your time and since you're obviously not in a hurry to get to work, Mrs.…?" He leaned forward, a look of expectancy on his face.

"Excuse me?!"

Oh no, he didn't!

"Not that it's any of your concern Detective, but it's Miz. Cole, not Mrs., and as a matter of fact I'm quite late for a very important meeting AND since I mostly keep to myself, while I certainly pray that poor woman's soul rests in peace, I seriously doubt there's anything of value I could contribute to your investigation. Good day!"

Not even waiting for his reaction, she swung her door shut and headed back to her room.

Chapter 2

Proverbs 3:5-6
Trust in the LORD with all thine heart; and lean not
unto thine own understanding
In all thy ways acknowledge Him, and He shall direct
thy paths...

Standing near the round conference table in her office as she finished up her financial presentation, Rissa cringed as Dan Eifel, the weatherman at her media house, suddenly waltzed through her door and spoke close at her shoulder. Literally. Since he was at least a half a foot shorter than her.

"So, Rissy…ready to take me up on that offer of dinner yet?" he drawled in his artificial, deep, 'I'm so sexy' voice. Plus, it just got under her skin the way he called her by that silly pet name.

Rissa heard his real voice during an earthquake a few months earlier and it had been at least four octaves higher. Like a girl, he'd screamed for his maker, dropped to his knees, and scrambled for cover beneath the nearest desk in the newsroom. Since then, she'd found it increasingly hard to keep a straight face whenever he spoke. And speaking of hard...good grief! What was that...pressed against her hip?!

Taking a hasty step forward and away from him, she turned back and pasted on as pleasant a smile as she could manage.

"No, afraid not, Dan. You know me, always busy working," she drew on her usual excuse.

"Oh, come on. You've gotta take a break some time." His smile was smarmy as he leered at her.

"Ally?" He turned to the Investment Manager and directed his question to her ample chest, which given her height and his lack of it, was right in his line of vision. "Am I right, or am I right?" he stepped forward; his nose practically nestled in her cleavage.

"Oh definitely," Ally made a face over his head and mouthed the word 'creep' as she also took a retreating step or two away from him, much to Rissa's amusement.

"You know what they say–all work and no play–"

"Make Rissa a stereotypical accountant," both Rissa and Ally chimed in chorus.

"That's right." He gave them an enthusiastic thumbs up.

"Rain check?" He directed his familiar weather pun to Rissa.

"Absolutely." She returned his hand gesture.

"Later, girls," he stared at Rissa and then winked as he finally quit her office.

Rissa took a seat behind her desk, regretting the HR open-door policy that allowed people like him to enter unannounced. This was getting out of hand. Normally his flirting was a mere annoyance, but this time felt different, that look he'd given her as he was leaving was a little scary.

"Can you believe him?" Ally barked out a laugh, as she dropped into one of the chairs around the conference table. "Someone should really report him to HR. Plus I am so sick of his oh-so-lame weather anecdotes and references. Maybe, he might actually have a shot at being likeable, if he was a few feet taller, less obnoxious, didn't get his clothing from the kid's department–"

Rissa's laugh turned into a snort.

"–and carried around a few tic-tacs." Ally ended.

"Onions, eww," they both said in stereo and then burst into even more raucous laughter.

"Wow." Ally wiped the moisture from her eyes as her laughter finally boiled down to a giggle or two.

"Bad-bad Ally." She slapped the top of her own hand. "That was not a very kind thing to say, but geez, why is it that people who are hygiene-challenged like that always want to get right up in your face?" She grimaced.

"I don't know, but be grateful, at least he didn't want to get right up on your butt."

"Nooh…you're kidding?" Ally gasped as she put a hand to her face.

"Oh yes, 'fraid so." Rissa sucked in a quick breath between pursed lips and nodded. "I mean the nerve of the guy, trying to cop a feel like that and with you standing right there. What did he think he could accomplish with a move like that anyway?"

"Well, it worked with Candy."

"Who? Oh, you mean the new girl." She snapped her fingers. "The general manager's admin assistant, right?"

"Yep, just last week. I believe her response went something like–ooh weatherman Dan–" Ally batted her eyes as her voice changed to a girly whine, "–I think I can feel a ridge of high pressure, moving in from the south."

"No way!" Rissa pushed back from her desk with a roar of laughter.

"Yes way! Would I lie to you?" Ally held her stomach as she laughed.

"I never thought it possible, but clearly, he's met his match–AKA someone who shares an affinity for quirky, inane weather humor. Just goes to show you, there's someone for everyone out there."

"Yeah, I guess."

The joviality of the moment slipped away and Rissa propped an elbow on her desk and rested her chin in her palm, as she wondered for the millionth time why that list didn't ever seem to include her.

"Ooh, I'm sorry honey." Concern shone in Ally's warm brown eyes. "Me and my big mouth. I didn't mean to upset you."

She and Ally had been friends for years, and though Ally had been happily married for five of them, Rissa had yet to meet her forever person.

"No, no, it's okay. I'm fine." She put on a carefree smile for her friend's benefit.

"I keep telling you, you've got to filter. You can't just say every thought that pops into your head. Most men don't like that."

"Well, I don't want 'most men.' Anyone worth having should be able to handle being challenged occasionally. Anyway, it's like I've said a hundred times—if I meet my person, it'll be great, and if I don't, well then, that's gonna be okay too."

"Let go and let God," they said almost simultaneously, sharing a smile.

"Actually...I've been meaning to ask you..." she rose from behind her desk and approached the conference table. "Would it be all right if I go to bible study with you next week?"

"Are you kidding me? Of course!" Ally leapt across the space between them and enveloped her in a bear hug. "Since you turned me down that first time I've been hoping and praying your heart would change for months. This is fantastic! You will not regret it, I promise you." Her eyes lit with joy. "It will transform your faith life." The gesture she made with her hands was expansive. "What in the world made you change your mind?"

"Well, some strange things have been happening lately. I left the grocery store on Saturday and on my way back to my car I was passing one of those huge delivery trucks parked halfway on the sidewalk. A couple of guys were lifting some big, heavy barrels off it and the next thing I knew, one of them just fell off."

"A man, or a barrel?"

"Seriously?"

"What?" Ally wiggled her eyebrows. "That could have been the start of a great love story."

Rissa ignored her. "Anyway…I don't think I've ever moved that fast in my life. I felt like I was airborne at some point. Plus, I've been having some strange dreams too."

"Really? Like what?"

"Aah…" Not sure how much she should share, she said, "I'm in strange places and I'm not sure how to explain it, but sometimes I feel a real presence of evil."

Ally's brows rose. Her face, a mask of concern.

"So anyway, I just have this feeling that maybe if I tap more into my spiritual side–"

Ally nodded.

"–I'll be better able to handle what's happening, or maybe figure out what I need to do. I dunno," she struggled with her thoughts, until an image of a smiling face above a big cardboard sign popped into her head. "I just think it's time to ramp up my prayer life."

"Absolutely, and don't you worry," Ally encircled her in another comforting hug. "God is great. There's no problem that faith won't solve and get you through it all."

"Amen to that." Rissa retook her seat, waved a hand over her desk, and brought her system back online.

"Now shoo," she pointed to the door. "We'll chat more next week. I've got to finish the presentation, and I have a ton of reports to get through. Plus, tomorrow's month-end Friday, so the payroll's due. Oh, and please close the door for me on your way out. Thanks!" She wanted no interruptions, from Dan or anyone else.

"Say no more," Ally jumped up. "You don't have to tell me twice, particularly when my money's involved." She blew her a kiss.

"Oh, and enjoy the Awards show tomorrow night, honey. I'm so jealous! See you when I see you," she sang as she headed out the door, and it slid closed behind her.

Chapter 3

Matthew 5:45
...for He maketh His sun to rise on the evil and on the good, and sendeth rain on the just and on the unjust...

Rissa took great care with her hair and make-up on Friday night. She was going to the planet's premier holo-event, her first ever, and she wasn't about to be found wanting while the entire world looked on.

She was one of the five lucky winners of a managers' door prize at their 2124 company awards ceremony at Christmas, and the gift was a very sought-after ticket to the 2125 International Academy Awards. She could scarcely believe it! Aside from the very healthy salary and attractive benefits package, working in a media house had certainly come with some exceptional perks.

The show that night was set to be spectacular. It was being advertised for weeks that for the first time ever, new, groundbreaking, cutting-edge technology designed by the defenders would be showcased. She'd never even seen one of their alien friends. They were notoriously clannish, keeping mostly to themselves, despite their significant influence on the global scene.

At the turn of the 22nd century they appeared– Verndari - the defenders. A race of humanoid aliens. They claimed they'd been living on earth, hiding in plain sight for decades and had stepped out of the shadows, once they determined that mankind was ready to accept them. She'd been very young when it happened, but she still remembered the excitement and buzz surrounding their arrival.

Given their advanced technology they'd quickly found their niche, becoming some of the wealthiest inhabitants of the planet. Plus, she'd heard rumors they all but controlled the progression, direction, and content of both social and mainstream media.

As invited guests from across the globe milled around the glittering theater lobby and adjoining rooms before the ceremony, they were treated to the sight of countless celebrities–real and digital. Stepping through the entryway, Rissa lost her breath as she looked up and around. The lobby was immense and from ceiling to floor the entire space had been transformed into an impressive holo-theatre with elaborate 2-D holograms. Some, larger than life, floated around near ceiling level, while others were stationary on the floor, sharing prepared presentations when someone approached. While off and on, others moved about the lobby floor in a set pattern. And even more remarkable were the solid 3-D renderings she discovered, as the night wore on. Their construct was immaculate. Their AI powered movements and highly intelligent, intuitive conversations were completely unpredictable, extraordinary, and awe-inspiring, as they greeted and chatted with specially invited guests as well as the real stars of stage and screen.

Glad she wasn't alone in her child-like wonder; she saw quite a few jaws drop and heard shouts of pleasure all around her as other guests shared in her excitement. She tried, she truly did, to look for some flaw that would give them away as fakes, but all such thought fled, as she basked in her five minutes of fame, after a camera drone captured her as she stepped forward to shake legendary 20th century actor, Sean Connery's hand.

"And who have we here'" the projected 3-D head of a popular British talk show host popped out to the left side of the drone.

"Hey Justin! I'm Alrissa." She nearly died on the spot.

"Well, Alrissa, here's your chance. The world is watching! What burning questions do you have for one Mr. Sean Connery?"

"Oh wow…ahh…first off, let me say this is so a-maz-ing!" She turned from the bobbing head and beamed at one of her very favorite actors of all time. "I wonder, do you know what an absolute icon you are in the world of filmmaking?" she said the first thing that popped into her mind and then hoped she hadn't made a complete idiot of herself before the millions watching.

"Well, I don't know about that, but I will say I'm an actor – it's not brain surgery," his R's rolled with his charming Scottish brogue. "People haven't asked for their money back, so I must be doing my job right." He winked, and she giggled like a schoolgirl– tickled by the humor of his quick wit.

"And thank you, Alrissa," he took her hand in both of his and held her gaze. "It's very kind of you to say. You know, fans like you, you're almost the only evidence that I exist."

That did it. She all but melted at his gracious words and like a child playing make-believe, in the little time she had left, she gave herself completely over to the sheer marvel of the once in a lifetime experience.

Clip-clop! Clip-clop!

All heads turned a few minutes later and loud gasps and then cheers rose as John Wayne - The

Duke, burst through a huge doorway and rode on a massive stallion, from one end of the lobby to the other and back, right above their heads.

"Look! Look!" A woman pointed across to the eastern side, up to the third floor as Marilyn Monroe smiled and waved from the brightly lit interior of a scenic elevator. It descended to the first floor and as she stepped out onto the open landing, just like in her famous 1955 film - *The Seven Year Itch*, the bottom of her beautiful, iconic white dress was lifted by blasts of air and her melodic laugh rang out, as she used her hands to maintain her modesty. This time the applause and screams of the very appreciative audience grew to a deafening roar.

Spotting Margot, her firm's Marketing Manager in the crowd, Rissa waved and made her way over for a quick chat, but she'd barely said hello when—

"Margot! Alrissa!"

They both turned. Rissa recognized the voice of the head of Consumer Relations who, just like her and Margot, had also been fortunate to win a coveted door prize.

"And who is that gorgeous hunk-a-chunk of burning love with her?" Margot licked her lips.

Rissa took him in—all six-foot plus of him. Blond, sinfully good looking and just impeccably dressed.

Oo-la-la...

Their colleague strutted over like a runway

model and was certainly dressed for the part in a skin-tight gold creation and eye-catching jewelry.

"Hey, Terri."

"Is this *the* most amazing night of your lives or what?" she gushed.

"Definitely." Margot nodded and graced Adonis with a blinding smile.

"It's just been one jaw-dropping experience after another." Rissa agreed. "Like nothing I could have ever imagined. I'm so glad we got to attend."

"Me too." Terri turned to her arm candy. "Oh, where are my manners? This is Svikari." She placed a possessive, well-manicured hand on his arm and smiled as she looked up into his eyes. "Meet Margot Channing and Alrissa Cole. They work at my firm."

"I'm Margot. Nice to see you." She rushed forward, almost spilling her drink in her haste to extend her hand for him to shake.

Rissa smiled and extended her hand next. "Hi, pleased to meet you."

He took it in a firm grip. "Likewise, Ms. Cole." His voice was rich and deep, with an odd accent she couldn't place.

"We just met in the holo-bar. He only drinks club soda. Can you imagine?" Terri giggled and gave him a playful slap on his arm.

"Oh, so you're a recovering alcoholic?" Rissa wondered out loud.

Terri gasped, while Margot made a choking

sound as she drank from her glass.

Svikari's eyebrows shot up in obvious surprise, but he recovered quickly.

"No…Ms. Cole. I actually just prefer it." His mouth curved into a very attractive half smile. "I've never had much of a taste for alcohol."

"Well, isn't that interesting. Neither do I." She returned his smile.

"Oh, and would you believe–" Terri rejoined the conversation with almost embarrassing eagerness and in an obvious ploy to turn their attention back to her, "–he's second generation Verndari."

Translation… Twice the money.

"Oh, is that right?" Rissa admired how he'd risen to her challenge. A weak-minded man would have taken offence at her query. *And* he was a defender. Now her interest was really piqued.

Margot however, she noticed, lost her bright smile. She even looked a bit pale.

"Excuse me, I…uh…need to visit the ladies' room." She hustled away.

"Well, that was odd. Anyhoo… Rissa, let me tell you all about how I plan to adapt some of this elaborate tech we're enjoying tonight for our customer experience program."

Nodding, Rissa stayed and chatted for a bit, or rather she listened to Terri pretty much dominate the conversation. And, as she observed her very first defender at close range, she couldn't shake the feeling there was something oddly familiar about him.

A musical note sounded around the lobby then, interrupting her musings and a voice invited everyone to head into the theatre since the main event was about to begin. Rissa took her assigned spot away from her four colleagues since they were not given seats together and as the evening wore on, she couldn't help but compare the tamer experience of the awards ceremony, with the spectacular opening in the lobby. Other than the selected stars who were the fortunate winners of the night, everyone else's response was far less enthusiastic than it had been earlier that night.

She stifled a yawn and looked at her watch.

10.30

No wonder. By this time, she'd have already been in bed. Well, it looked like the show was almost over. From the electronic program projection in front of her she could see there was only one more award to be handed out.

She was about to test her theory that since everyone was in the theatre she could probably sneak out to the lobby and then her car, when–

CONGRATULATIONS ALRISSA COLE YOU'RE A WINNER!

–popped up in flashing red letters surrounded by exploding fireworks on the little table in front of her seat. At the same time a voice came over the public address system and announced that anyone who received the message had won a special lottery that entitled them to enter a very special game room with an opportunity to win fabulous prizes, to end their already fabulous night. Her curiosity trumped thoughts of sleep ; Rissa joined the other lottery winners in the cheery game room.

There were probably two dozen tables and at each, four celebs were already seated. The game was simple–three of the celebs were 3-D fakes and only one was the real deal. Three of the lottery winners were to sit at each table and then were given five minutes to chat with the celebs after which they had to guess which was the real flesh and blood one.

An attendant called her name to usher her to her seat and as she followed him, she heard 'Jeff Merit' and 'Margot Channing.'

"I wonder what the prizes are?" Margot took her seat, right next to Rissa. "And both of us from the same company? What are the odds?"

"I know, really random, right?" She returned her smile.

The allotted time for chatting began and was over so quickly that Rissa seriously doubted she could make the correct choice. It was like meeting Sean Connery all over again, except worse, these were all 22nd century stars. Not a deceased one among them.

The lights snapped off and there was a collective

gasp across the room as for a few moments they sat in pitch blackness. Then a spotlight illuminated a table to her left and the star directly under it flickered like a glitch in a bad computer program and disappeared. More gasps, some applause and an expletive filled the room. One by one in rapid succession the spotlight hopped from table to table and fake stars were eliminated. The noise in the room rose as celebration and discussion broke out at the tables where lottery winners learned if they had guessed correctly.

Only two were left and they were at Rissa's table. Fingers crossed she'd picked the right one. Her choice across the table lit up and he evaporated.

Damn!

Margot grabbed her arm.

The lights came up.

And all hell broke loose.

Chapter 4

Numbers 35:30
Whoso killeth any person, the murderer shall be put to death by the mouth of witnesses…

Attendants ushered everyone from the game room out into the large lobby just as the staccato tones of a synthesized voice came over the PA system.

"We do apologize for any inconvenience, but please be advised that given the circumstances, we have summoned the relevant authorities, and you will be required to meet with their representative before you are permitted to depart. When you hear your name, please follow the holo-signs, and proceed promptly to conference room D. As you wait for your turn, please enjoy a complimentary cocktail of your choice at the bar. Again, we do apologize for any inconvenience."

The message started repeating and Rissa was about to join the throng of patrons who'd already made a B-line for the bar when she spied some activity at the entrance to the lobby. It looked like a couple people were meeting with two uniformed theatre officials.

Wait…is that…? Oh no!

What were the odds that of all the detectives, they'd send him. The theatre wasn't even anywhere near the NYPD's 15th precinct.

She couldn't be sure from this distance, so she channeled her inner sneaky-spy and moved in as close as she dared, to see if it was really her unwelcome morning visitor.

Standing behind an oversized 2-D holo of ground-breaking Star Trek actress Nichelle Nichols at her Lt. Nyota Uhura best, she used it as camouflage and peered across the lobby to the entryway.

Sure enough, there he was.

Without the haze of anger that had clouded her vision at their first meeting she was able to appreciate the view this time. He looked like he was in his late thirties, probably just shy of six feet and though not classically handsome, he was quite attractive with dark blonde hair. She admired the cut of his navy trousers as well as his choice of color coordination in a classic white sweater that hugged his pecs and biceps like a second skin as he removed and slung his matching navy jacket over a muscled shoulder.

As luck would have it, he turned in her direction, just as Lt. Uhura flickered. The back of the holo became the front as it walked right through her, as she too spun about. Thankful for her choice of pairing moderately high heels with her evening gown that night, she walked quickly away, towards the ladies' room.

About halfway through a glass of the best tropical fruit punch she'd had in her life–

"Alrissa Cole. Alrissa Cole, please proceed to Conference room D."

Typical.

Rissa made like a vacuum cleaner of old and sucked up as much of her drink as she could, before sliding off the bar stool to follow the line of flashing red arrows moving along the walls of the lobby.

She still couldn't believe it. She'd just watched Margot die, right in front of her. She'd thought maybe it was a heart attack, given the way she collapsed, but now, as she walked on her way to meet with the police, she wondered if there was more to it. She knew they had to investigate unexpected deaths. So, given her proximity to the incident, did that mean she was now a possible suspect, if it turned out to be foul play?

Walking down a series of corridors, she came to

the appointed door.

"Okay, you can do this. You can do this," she bolstered her courage by repeating the positive affirmation under her breath as she listened to the AI announce her.

The door slid open with a slight whistle.

"Well, hello Detective. Didn't think I'd be seeing you again." She entered the cozy meeting room and extended her hand as she walked over to where he stood, awaiting her

"Miz. Cole?" He put the same emphasis on her title as she had done the week before. "I thought that was you I saw out in the lobby. Wow. I gotta say, you clean up real good." His voice was a deep velvet trap, as his warm blue gaze ran over her from head to toe, much the same as the week before, though eliciting very different feelings in her tonight.

She felt her face heat at the blatant interest in that gaze, the unexpected pleasure of his warm touch and the tenor of his voice, as he delivered the compliment.

He released her hand and cleared his throat. "Please have a seat, he indicated one of the two plush chairs at the front of a small metal table "Water?" He walked around to the back, sat, then leaned to his right and grasped the handle of an elegant glass pitcher sitting on an equally tasteful side table.

"No, thank you," she shook her head.

He filled the tumbler in front of him, raised it to

his lips and took a long swallow. "So basically, I'm going to ask you about what happened tonight." He placed the glass back on the desk in front of him. "As I started to explain when last we met…" the left side of his mouth twitched upward, "…we've unfortunately had a rash of strange deaths of young women recently, so although this venue is some distance away from the primary site, we just need to rule out any possibility this incident tonight was related. Hopefully this time, I'll actually *get* to ask you the questions."

No twitch, this time. This time she was treated to the full one-hundred-watt brilliance of his smile.

And it annoyed the heck out of her.

She had intended to avoid mentioning their first encounter at all costs. Obviously, it was too much to hope he'd be decent enough to do the same. Thinking of how best to navigate the waters in which she now found herself, she got set to be contrite.

"Yes, well, about that. I feel like I should apologize for my behavior–"

"No, you don't." He grinned.

"Excuse me?"

"You and I both know you don't "feel like you should." In fact, I'm willing to bet you still think you were completely justified in slamming your door in my face. It's more likely you hoped I wouldn't call you out on your conduct. That I'd be…a gentleman. Just one problem with that plan…" he leaned forward, softened his voice, as though sharing a secret, "…I'm not."

Really?

Who IS this guy?

She tucked a couple loose strands of hair that brushed her cheek behind her ear, feeling like she was under a microscope. But she recovered quickly and met his penetrating gaze head on.

"Hmm…interesting theory. I didn't realize behavioral science was a part of the required training at the police academy, Detective."

She lowered her voice an octave. "Or do you just enjoy watching all those 21st Century series about Quantico, like I do?"

He laughed out loud, then shook his head as his humor faded.

They sat in silence for a moment.

Leaning back in his chair he gave her a look–all intriguing intent. Like he wanted to say something that had nothing to do with his investigation.

"Okay, let's get right to it then, shall we?"

And just like that…the moment passed.

"Just answer to the best of your recollection."

"Sure." She nodded.

He looked down at the desk, flipped a page on a pad of paper and clicked the end of an old writing instrument he was holding in his hand.

"Wow. You use a notepad and pen?"

"Uh yeah–" he glanced down at the articles she

referenced, "–I guess I'm kinda old-school like that. Unheard of these days, right?" He flashed a now familiar smile.

"Pretty much." She pointed to the pen and held out her hand. "May I?"

He hesitated for a long second then, "Sure." He handed it over.

It was silver, sleek. The weight and smoothness of it between her fingers as well as the lingering warmth from his grip felt somehow familiar and comforting. "Very nice." She handed it back. "I see why you like it."

"Really?" His brows rose. "Sometimes I think I was born in the wrong century. Most people take one look and then berate me with a litany of why an electronic note-taker would be a far better choice, given my profession."

They both chuckled.

"But not you." He sobered.

"No…not me." She met his warm gaze.

The left side of his mouth inched up. "Okay." His head tilted to the side, then he looked down at his notepad. "So, how do you know the deceased?"

He was all business again.

"I worked with her. But you already knew that, didn't you?"

He glanced up. "Which company?"

Okay, so it's like that, is it?

"Kittridge and Clemens Media." She played

along.

"And what was her position there?"

"She's–uh–or rather was…the Marketing Manager."

"And you?"

"I'm the CFO."

His head jerked up.

Genuine ignorance this time?

"Really? You don't look like an Accountant."

"Oh? And what in your estimation *should* an Accountant look like, Detective?"

He chuckled, looked down, rubbed a hand over his chin, then met her gaze again.

"Okay, you've got me there. So, were you lady's friends? Hang out together much?"

"No, not really. We'd exchange a word here and there over coffee, or lunch, but I wouldn't say we were friends."

"Did you know, or hear anything about her personal life? Like did she ever mention any boyfriend, or husband troubles? Anyone unusual ever come by the office to see her?"

"No, no, and no."

His left eyebrow arched upward.

"What can I say?" She shrugged. "I'm sorry I can't be of more help. Other than in the break room and at team meetings, I rarely saw her. She worked on the fourth floor. I'm on the fifth. Like I said, we weren't friends. Plus, my workload is beyond crazy.

I have absolutely no time for office gossip."

He jotted something down.

"What about tonight? I saw from the seating chart for the bonus game, you guys were placed right next to each other. Anything you can remember about the moments before she died?" His gaze sharpened on her. "She say anything unusual to you?"

"It was just crazy, what happened. She seemed fine at first when I saw her earlier in the lobby. Better than fine actually."

"How so?"

"Another colleague of ours introduced us to a defender she picked up at the holo-bar and at first Margot was practically salivating over him. He was mega-gorgeous. I mean… wow… Face like an angel. Tall. Just impeccably dressed and muscled. Built like a GQ-holo."

"That type appeals to you, does it?" His tone was dry.

"Looking like that, *and* he's an ultra-rich defender? He's every single, straight woman on the planet's type, Detective."

She couldn't be sure, but she thought he looked a bit peeved at her response.

"So, you said "at first" she was salivating." He flipped back a page in his notes. "What happened to change that?"

"I dunno, like I said, it was strange. She was all

smiles and giggles after she was introduced to him, at least until Terri said he was a defender, then she got pale and quiet and left for the ladies' room."

"So, this defender, did you catch his name, or were you too distracted by all his muscles?"

The skin above his jawline jumped.

Yep, peeved.

"Ahh-hem," she masked the laugh that bubbled up by clearing her throat. "Svikari? I think that's what Terri called him. She all but dominated the conversation, so he really didn't say very much. Oh, I remember he mentioned he was in PR."

"Okay." He scribbled furiously in his notepad. "And what about in the game room?"

"Well, we chatted with each of the celebs at the table. Come to think of it, she started out all gung-ho and then she sort of got distracted. I thought it was just a strategy, you know, to listen more intently to the celeb's responses and just let me and the other guy ask all the questions. Before long, time was up, and we used our keypads to choose the one we thought wasn't a holo. They got down to the last two who happened to be at our table, I felt her grab my arm in the dark, I figured in excitement, but then the lights came up and she was kind of clutching at her chest, then she just collapsed."

"With which hand?"

"Uh…both I think.

"Yeah, both," she confirmed, as a picture of the

horrible moment replayed in her mind's eye.

"Poor soul." Rissa felt a swell of pity. "She was so young. It's just so tragic."

He nodded, answering sympathy in his eyes.

"Now I remember it, I don't even think she cried out. And then the attendants rushed over to see what happened and tried to help and made everyone stay back, so if she said anything at the end, I'm afraid I didn't hear it."

He nodded and wrote something else in his notes.

"Well, from all I've heard so far, I think she likely died from natural causes, but we'll know more once the tox screen, skin analysis and such come back with the medical examiner's report. In the meantime, please call the precinct if you think of anything else, anything at all you think might be pertinent to the case."

He rose and she did as well, taking his cue that their little meeting was at an end.

"Thank you, for your cooperation." He extended his hand across the table.

"Sure." She shook it, enjoying the pleasant warmth of his grasp one last time.

"Actually–" he touched the top of his wristwatch a couple times, and she got an immediate close proximity alert on hers, "–call me, anytime, day or night. My contacts are all in there."

"What...no call card?"

He looked confused.

"Given your affinity for paper…I thought for sure you'd be handing out those little cardboard thingies I've seen on display at the museum of ancient and modern history." She flashed him a sultry smile.

His smile was slow. Provocative. His gaze…back to intriguing, smoky blue intent.

She turned and headed for the door.

"You stay safe and blessed Detective." She glanced back at him over her shoulder, as the door slid open.

"You do the same, Miz. Cole."

As the door whistled closed behind her, Duncan suppressed the urge to release a low and very primitive growl.

"This one's gonna be the death of me."

Shaking his head, he tapped a button on the room's virtual intercom to alert the AI he was ready to see the next person.

Chapter 5

Colossians 1:16
For by Him were all things created, that are in heaven,
and that are in earth, visible and invisible, whether they
be thrones, or dominions, or principalities, or powers ...

On Thursday of the following week, Duncan was sitting in the 15th precinct squad room when one of only two female detectives on the team walked in with news on the two most recent mysterious deaths.

"Here they are, results hot off the press, from the ME. For the Tower Heights and the Holoworld Theatre game room vics." Detective Danielle Almonzo motioned him over, as well as the other detective on the case. She threw the data dots up on the squad room case wall and expanded them, two holos wobbled and then settled side by side into clear view.

Duncan rose from his seat and joined her at the wall.

"Okay, let's see what we've got." He scrolled through a few screens on the Tower Heights case first. "So, this one matches with the M O on the bodies of the other murder victims," he pointed to the other five that were already up on the left side of the wall.

"No marks of violence, and it's consistent in terms of the shattering of multiple bones of the neck and upper vertebrae." He flipped through the report again. "Says here it would take tremendous force suddenly pressing the bones of the spine together to cause those burst fractures, breaking the neck in many places at the same time."

"Well, I'm no doctor…" Almonzo paused, as a flicker of pain crossed her features. "But, with that level of force, shouldn't there be some contusions or something? Even punctured skin?"

"Yeah, that'd be my guess. Hey, you okay Monzo?" Duncan wondered about the cause of the hurt he'd seen reflected in her expression.

"Huh?" She turned to face him fully, "Oh yeah, never better."

She gave him a smile that didn't quite reach her eyes, but he let it go.

"Okay, what about the game room vic?" he

wondered.

She rifled through the e-files, selected one image, and expanded it with her thumb and forefinger. "Same."

"How is that even possible though?" Detective Robert Dorran left his seat and joined the discussion. He propped a hip on the edge of the nearest desk. "We reviewed the footage from the game room dozens of times and nothing. One minute she's fine and the next she's on the floor. Multiple witnesses at the table and the ones nearby all said the same thing– she clutched her chest like a heart attack."

"But with both hands like that though?" Almonzo pulled a chair out from behind the same desk Dorran was leaning on and sat down. "Just follow me here. Wright, come at me like you're gonna strangle the life outta me."

"Thought you'd never ask." Duncan's quick response earned him a high five from Dorran and a few raucous comments and laughter from the other guys within earshot in the squad room.

"Yeah, yeah, tell it to your mothers." Almonzo had her own quick comeback.

"Okay, so like this?" Duncan leaned down and put his hands around her slender neck.

She pulled his forearms down a bit to rest on her chest. "Best you ever had, right? Don't get used to it."

"Yeah, you wish." He chuckled.

She slumped in the chair and leaned back. "Dorran, you getting this?"

He moved around to the back of the desk and pulled up a small camera, angled the lens in their direction, and hit a button. "Okay, go."

"So," she grabbed Duncan's forearms and wrists with a surprising grip, he thought, given her slim frame, and simulated what a civilian without self-defense training might try to do to escape his hold. "I know this is waaay out there, like Neptune out there, but what if she wasn't clutching her chest. What if…she was really clawing at something *on* her chest."

"Okay, I see where you're going." Dorran flicked off the camera, pulled out the data dot, and put it on his desk holo maker. He pulled the screen towards him. "What happens if I doctor the image to remove Wright's arms?"

After manipulating the image, he got up and handed the dot to Almonzo who hopped off the chair and stood at the wall once again.

She threw the video up with the others, chose a spot, and froze the image. "And now the footage from the game room." She rifled through the screens, selected one, pulled it out and drew it across until it was right next to the other one. "Et voila, as the French would say."

Dorran came over and expanded the images even more.

"Well, I'll be a monkey's uncle." He stepped back and leaned against the front of his desk.

"Yes, you are." Almonzo grinned. "So, barring the slight difference in the angle…"

"They're almost exactly the same," Duncan finished her sentence.

"I had a dog and buh-buh-bingo was his name!" She slapped Duncan on the back.

"But what about the level of force?" Dorran asked. "You just said it had to be major, right? Could a person do that?"

Duncan and Almonzo both turned in his direction.

"We're lookin' at the freakin' invisible man over here–" Almonzo pointed to the wall, "–and that's the big question on your mind right now?" She shook her head at him. Looking back at the wall, she groaned and put a hand to her head.

Could it be? They were looking for an invisible unsub?

Duncan echoed Almonzo's groan and rubbed a hand over tired eyes and then across his chin. Mentally, he prepared to face what was shaping up to be the toughest case of his career.

<hr>

Chapter 6

<hr>

Genesis 1:16
And God made two great lights; the greater light to rule
the day, and the lesser light to rule the night; He made
the stars also ...

"What? What's all this?" Rissa looked to her younger sister Summer for a response as she pointed at the bent heads and even sadder faces of her niece and nephew, as she ushered them all into her foyer early on Saturday morning.

"Oh, they're just sulking cause they're missing a school field trip to that new holo-park. Their class is going from this afternoon until tomorrow morning. I'm so sorry to do this to them. They've been looking forward to it for months. Not that we'd even let them, but they can't go without an adult. The teachers were very clear they're only there to provide limited guidance on the different nature trails."

"Well, couldn't you or Brad skip the work thing?" Both Summer and her husband worked for the same ad firm.

"Nope, we can't get out of it. We're still working on that very important, very fussy client's campaign I told you about. We stay till we're done, so it's def gonna be an all-nighter. Which is why I need you to babysit."

"Okay, gotcha."

Rissa felt a tug on her fingers and a tiny sticky hand grasped hers. She looked down and seven-year-old Sarah's tear-filled green eyes filled her vision and her heart.

"Couldn't you take us, Auntie Risha?" She had an adorable little lisp so her pronunciation of Rissa's name always came out with an 'h' instead of an 's'.

A look at her one-year-older brother Sam showed he wasn't handling their disappointment any better.

"Sure, why not." She gave Sarah's hand a reassuring squeeze. It's not like she had anything else to do. A trip to the grocery store was looking to be the highlight of her weekend. "I can take them, Summer. Besides, it sounds like great fun! I've heard the 3-D rendering of the animals is amazing."

"Are you sure?" Her sister grasped her arms and

looked directly into her eyes. "They're getting to be a real handful you know."

"No worries," Rissa waved away her concern.

"Yes, please, Mom. Pleeease?" the kids begged in unison.

"All right, but only if, you're sure."

"Yay!" As children tend to do, they made a complete three-sixty. Tears dispelled, they held hands as they happily jumped up and down.

"Hey! Hey! Hey!" She gave them a look, and they immediately quieted. "Best behavior for Auntie Rissa, you two," she put on what Rissa called her 'Mom voice.' "I mean it." She pointed a forefinger at each in turn.

"Yes Mom." Subdued, but still smiling, they promptly sat on the floor already distracted with a hand-held game Sam was holding.

"Okay, well I've got to get going. Thank you so much sweetie." They embraced and then she leaned down and planted a kiss on each child's head. "Love you all," she sang as she headed out the door.

Rissa waved to Brad as he waited in the car. She closed the door "Okay, so who wants pancakes with fresh strawberries and whipped cream, while I get packed up for our little adventure?"

"Me! Me! Me!" They nearly knocked her over as they leapt up off the floor and continued jumping as they held onto her.

"Okay, okay," she laughed. "Come on

munchkins." Putting a hand on each of their backs she ushered them into the kitchen.

———•●•———

After a near two-hour drive, they arrived at the holo-park and were immediately thrown into a whirlwind of activities. There was registration with the park's customer care reps and then they assembled with all the other families, teachers, and park guides, as they began their exploration.

First, they walked the nature trails. The teachers were quite knowledgeable, and parents and kids alike learned almost as much from them as the park guides.

Then there were the many different petting zoos. And Alrissa didn't know if she or Sam was the most excited about the Jurassic zone where they got to see 3-D dinosaurs up close.

None of the animals were real, so there was this super-safe safari of lions, tigers, zebras, giraffes, and so many others, where they were able to freely observe the habits of all the animals, some long extinct and gone from the jungles of the world.

Last, they headed to the aquatic center where they could see and even swim with dolphins, whales and all kinds of water dwellers. There were also mythical sea creatures, like the Loch Ness monster.

That night, after having only a light lunch on the

nature trails, their delicious dinner seemed like a veritable outdoor feast of barbecued chicken, with potato salad, burgers, and hot dogs, and of course, campfire smores for dessert. Then they were shown to the resting area so they could end their wonderful adventure by sleeping out in tents under the stars.

"Hey Summer," Rissa called her sister right after dinner.

"What's wrong? Did something happen?"

"No, no," she was quick to allay the anxiety she saw on Summer's face and heard ringing in her voice. "We're having a great time. This place is amazing! You should see it." She held up her wrist and tried to give her sister a view of her surroundings.

A small 3D version of Summer's bobbing head turned from left to right just above her wristwatch. "Can't see a thing sis–" she squinted, "–next time maybe give me the tour in daylight."

"Oh gosh, of course, it's too dark. Silly me." Rissa giggled. "Oh, and about that, we're getting ready to turn in for the night, and the kids wanna have a sleep over of sorts in their friend Zoe and her parents' tent. Do you know them?"

"Oh yeah, we do sleepovers with the Ashleys all the time. They're great people."

"Oh, cool. So, you're okay with it?"

"Oh yeah, absolutely."

"All righty then. What about you? How's the

project coming?"

"Exhausting, but it'll all be worth it when I'm driving to the mall in our new Mercedes," Summer sang, referring to the large purchase Rissa knew she and Brad were hoping to make with the bonus they'd receive if the campaign went as intended.

"Sweeeet," they both said and then laughed.

"Okay, see you tomorrow."

"Have a great night! Bye-e!" Summer's image faded and then disappeared.

Rissa got the kids organized for their sleepover then headed back to her own tent for the night. She checked the time and saw it was almost 9pm. No doubt she'd be asleep by 9.30.

"Way to go Rissa. Oh, what an exciting life you do lead," she said under her breath.

Aside from being spaced apart for privacy, the interior of each tent was well appointed. This was definitely not your parents Friday night down at the lake, being eaten alive by mosquitoes, kind of situation.

Oh no, this was luxury camping.

What did they call it in the 21st century? Glamping?

All open plan, it was a combination bedroom and sitting room. She noticed a fair-sized seating area on the right with adjustable lighting making it a cozy nook to curl up and read an e-book, or, as she'd seen in the Ashleys tent, the couch also unfolded into a large bed where at least four kids could sleep. On the left there was even a little two-drawer chest for storage and a bedside table with a brightly illuminated clock.

And that bed…

A large, very comfortable looking one dominated the back left corner of the tent.

Yep, after the most active day she'd had in years she was going to sleep like a log in that.

Look up… whispered through her mind.

"Wow…" she gasped.

A large opening in the top of the tent, shielded by some kind of shimmering force-field, gave her a breathtaking view of the deep, dark night sky, illuminated with dozens of twinkling stars.

It was a sobering and timely revelation, given all the fake constructs surrounding her in the holo-park that afternoon. There was absolutely nothing to compare to the glory of God's creation. Everything else was just pretense.

Yes, she would sleep very well indeed with such a powerful reminder she was always under the watchful gaze of the one who created such an awe-inspiring vista.

Chapter 7

Hebrews 10:24-25
And let us consider one another to provoke unto love
and to good works: Not forsaking the assembling of
ourselves together, as the manner of some is; but
exhorting one another…

"Rissa…"

She heard a whisper of her name and the end of her own sharp intake of breath as she woke.

In a sleep fog, her mind tried to make sense of what her eyes were seeing in the strange surroundings. She took in the seating area and the tent entrance and remembered where she was.

Had she been travelling again? She had the vague feeling someone was watching her.

Wait.

Her gaze flew back to the tent entrance, and she noticed with considerable alarm that it was open. Had she forgotten to close it before turning in that night? A glance at the clock on the bedside table told her it was just after 11pm, so at least she hadn't spent the entire night with it open. She rose from the bed, intending to close it, but took no more than two steps when something that looked like a large black panther appeared at the entrance, looked in at her and began a slow approach.

What in the world?

Okay, stay calm, she thought, as she kept a sharp eye on it, or as sharp as she could, given the dimness of the interior of the tent, illuminated only by a watery moon.

As far as she knew, all the animals on the compound were 3-D generated, so this must just be some new and exciting element of the safari, albeit a huge miscalculation in her estimation.

She got no further with that thought and shrieked as the creature bared its teeth and sprang forward. But it never reached her. From between the spread fingers of hands she'd unconsciously held up to shield herself, she saw an enormous, unusual-looking white wolf rear up on its hind legs and begin to tangle with the feline. The skirmish was over in scant seconds as the cat broke free, raced to the tent opening and melted into the night.

Wow! She felt like applauding. She hadn't even seen where the wolf came from. This tech was really amazing and starting to rival the production at the International Academy Awards. Scary as all hell, but fantastic, nonetheless.

The wolf stood for a moment, looked to the tent entrance and then back at her. Then it began to walk towards her, the steady almost rhythmic rise and fall of its shoulders and haunches mesmerizing in the moonlight. It was huge indeed. Waist high, it stopped mere inches away and instead of fear, she felt a strange connection to it, as she stared into its piercing, bright blue eyes.

She reached out, slowly, and when it didn't move; she ran gentle fingers along its furry back.

Like silk and velvet…

She thought it leaned into her touch, but as she reached out again it turned away and ran back to the entrance, gave her a last look, and then disappeared into the darkness, leaving her feeling strangely alone.

The next morning before they left, she stopped to talk to one of the customer care staff she saw after breakfast and inquired about the unexpected element of the park's attractions she'd experienced the night before.

"You know…the huge white wolf, tangling with a big black cat? I think it was a panther. And then the wolf chased it away?" She explained when the young man looked perplexed at her inquiry.

"I mean, certainly it was exciting, but I'm not really sure it's for everyone, so just saying–" she held up her open palms in a gesture of surrender, "–you might want to rethink it going forward."

"Excuse me Miss, but we don't have any programming like that near the dwellings. All the holo-animals are set up in the designated safari area and the petting zoos."

Huh?

"So, what you're saying is, it was all real? I could have died petting that thing?!" She felt sick, and like she was about to hyperventilate and throw up, all at the same time. "Young man, those animals are just a lawsuit in the making!"

"Ma'am–?"

He had the required "the customer is always right" smile on his face, but she could tell he was annoyed. And grr! When did she go from being a Miss to a Ma'am? Again!

"–Petting… what… *thing*?" He spoke slowly, as one might to a child, or someone who didn't understand English very well.

"Listen up–" she read the electronic name tag glowing on his chest, "–Chad. The white wolf? Last night? In my tent? Haven't you been paying attention to a word I said?"

"To my knowledge there are no real animals on the compound, so maybe you were dreaming?"

"Excuse me?!"

"So, if there's nothing else I can help you with before you leave, thank you for visiting our Holo-Park. Have a great holo-day!" He put on a bright smile to go with the tagline, turned on his heel and briskly walked away.

"Oh, the nerve of that guy!" She'd have a great day all right, already planning to give 'Chad' a very special review, she called out to the kids who were saying goodbye to their friends and guided them out to the car park.

She got them and all their souvenirs from their great adventure packed into the car and as she started up the engine and started to pull out of the spot, a call came through.

"Hey, Summer, we're on our way back to you now. Should be there in an hour."

"Uh…about that…"

She knew her sister's tone meant something was up. "What is it?" she droned.

"Well, we just need a little more time to finish the pitch before we can get back home, so can you please just keep them for a couple more hours?"

"I guess so, sure."

"And could you also please just take them to the 10.30am service at my church? They're about to take first communion, so they can't miss any Sunday school. I packed some nice clothes they can wear, just in case, thanks so much, Bye-e!"

Click.

All without taking a breath. Rissa shook her head and smiled as she reversed and then switched off the engine of the car. Good thing *she'd* packed a nice dress 'just in case.' "Okay, come on munchkins, you heard your mom. Let's see if we can get a complimentary tent to change into our Sunday best. We're going to church."

After the service, Rissa thanked the Reverend as he wished her a blessed week. She'd only been to her sister's church a few times, since they lived so far apart, but she always enjoyed the style of preaching there.

"Okay guys, hand them over," she held out her palms for the snack wrappers the kids were still holding from the munchies they'd enjoyed during Sunday school, as they climbed into the back seat of the car and got strapped in.

"Sam…you finished with that?" she pointed to the nearly empty juice bottle he was also trying to balance in his tiny hands. He nodded.

"Okay, let me take that for you." She grabbed both the bottle and the wrappers and looked along the sidewalk for a garbage receptacle. Why was there never one of those public mini trash compactors around when you needed one. She walked to the back of the car, thought the word 'open', and the energy field that protected the car from collision damage flickered for a moment, then disappeared. The trunk slid up and she placed the stuff in a small trash bag she kept in the corner.

She'd just reclosed the trunk when–

"Oh!" She cried out as she stumbled to the left, her feet came off the ground and the next thing she knew she was falling, right into the wide roadway–

Oh God...help me!

–And into the path of an oncoming car.

She cried out again as, in the nick of time, she felt strong arms stop her fall and sweep her backward and up against the back bumper of her car.

"Dear God, are you okay?"

"Uh yeah, I think so. Oh wow..." She gripped her rescuer's nicely muscled arm with one hand and put the other to her chest trying to catch her breath. A quick glance through the SUV's back window confirmed that fortunately the kids were too enthralled with their game pads to notice what happened.

"Thank you, so much Detective." She released him and pushed away from the car as he pulled back, giving her space. "What in the world? I don't even want to think what might have happened if you hadn't been here."

Wait. Why *was* he here?

"I mean, what are the chances? Where in the world did you come from?"

"I was walking to my car when I noticed you, so I was coming over to say hello when you started to fall. I just got out of service." He pointed back to church.

"You're kidding? So did I."

"Really?" He looked pleased. "You go to this church?"

"Oh, no." She shook her head. "I go to St. Peter's near my home. I'm just here today to do my sister a favor. I brought my niece and nephew to Sunday school."

"Oh." He nodded.

They stood in silence for a long moment.

Her mind slid back to her stumble. Near-death experience aside, the brief feeling of being in his strong, steely arms had been pretty darn hot!

"Ah...Okay." She was the first to break the silence that suddenly felt awkward. "I've got to get these two back home to their mom and dad. Thanks again for saving my life Detective." She extended her hand, and he took it in his warm grasp. "You stay safe and blessed this week."

"You too, Miz Cole."

She waved as she slowly pulled away from the curb. In her rearview, she saw him still standing there unmoving, his face a mask of...questioning concern...?

———•●•———

Duncan stood there until he lost sight of her SUV as it turned a corner.

He released a shaky breath.

He still didn't quite know what to make of it himself, and he certainly wasn't going to say anything to her. Wouldn't know what, or how to say it actually. Well, at least not without sounding completely insane.

That from his vantage point, it looked just like she'd been pushed.

Chapter 8

Matthew 7:7
Ask, and it shall be given you; seek, and ye shall find;
knock, and it shall be opened onto you…

Back at his desk in the squad room bright and early on Monday morning Duncan thought about how best to introduce the subject of what he'd seen the day before. Figuring it was probably best to just jump right in, he took the plunge.

"Something happened yesterday. Don't know what to make of it. I saw one of the women I interviewed for the Channing case. She was standing behind her car and next thing I knew; it looked like she just listed to the side, then levitated about six inches off the ground before falling sideways into oncoming traffic.”

“Levitated?” Dorran sat up in his chair. “You mean like jumped, right?”

“No, sir. I mean lifted off the ground real smooth-like.”

“And you had how many drinks before this?” Almonzo snorted.

“Not even a sip of water, Monzo. I’d just got out of church.”

“Church?! You go to church? You gotta be kidding me.”

“Oh, we don’t got enough hours in the day to unpack this one.” Dorran leaned back in his chair as he clasped his hands behind his head.

“Take your best shot.” Duncan held up his hands in surrender. “But there’s nothing either one of you can say that could make me lose my walk. The love of the Lord is a powerful and beautiful thing, my friends. You should try it.”

Dorran shrugged his acceptance, but Almonzo looked uncomfortable. Such a look of sadness flashed across her lovely face and within her soft hazel-hued eyes that he could see a little shepherding of her in his future. This wasn’t the first time he’d seen indications of a painful past that needed healing, with her and with others he knew, so he shelved the thought away for another, more opportune time.

“Anyway, what I saw makes me think there may be something to Monzo’s invisible unsub theory.”

"Aw, hehll no," she shook her head, "uh-uh, I'm done." She put her hands up, just as he had done moments before. "Now I know good and well you not trying to put that mess on me? That's a twenty-four hour hold in a psych ward, *with* a Thorazine drip, for real, Detective."

Dorran laughed and reached across his desk to hers for a fist bump. "I heard that."

Duncan chuckled. "Well maybe not an unsub exactly." He stood up and strolled over to the case wall. "Just hear me out. Hypothetically, if it were possible–" he reached for one of the small interface discs they kept in a container near the wall that allowed them to work more intimately with the precinct's AI - Security and Intelligence System. He pressed it onto his left temple, "–what would we be looking at? What invisible force could make a person lift off the ground like that? I know a hovercraft uses blowers to produce a large volume of air, like a cushion underneath and then it just floats along on top. So, maybe this was some kind of focused airfield, coming up from beneath her feet?"

His thoughts became a summary of salient points on the electronic wall, the beginnings of a grocery list of possibilities, just as a computer-generated female voice said, "Searching…There is no record of any such adaptation of a hovercraft's apparatus."

Dorran shrugged, joined him at the wall and put

on the interactive tech. "What about some kind of new drone that can displace energy maybe?"

"Searching…There is no record of any machine, or weapon, capable of energy displacement on such a small scale."

"And you're both wrong." Monzo waved them out of her way as she grabbed a disc and touched her temple. "Every piece of tech on the planet for the last twenty-five years has either been designed, or altered by a defender. If this invisibility theory is legit then I'm willing to bet my butt this is one of them in some kinda camouflage, or something.

"SiS, access case file MC three fifty-nine, dash twenty-three, o-two, twenty-five and pull the game room footage."

"Accessing." A blur of people and 3-D holos moving around the room raced across the case wall.

"Now, look for any residual energy trail…parameters - table number twenty, time of death - Channing…Margot."

"Energy signature detected." A faint red trail appeared like a haze next to where Margot was seated.

"Okay, now perform a spectral analysis."

"Analyzing…Scan shows trace elements of unknown origin, also non-human signature–probability 98% alien species known as Verndari."

"Which church did you say you went to yesterday? And around what time 'd you get out?"

She pointed at Duncan without taking her eyes off the virtual wall.

"St. Theresa's on Freemont. Maybe noon, I guess."

"SiS, search traffic cams for Detective Duncan Wright."

"Searching." A series of pictures of the street outside the church from all different vantage points and distances flicked by at a rapid rate. "Located."

They pulled a couple different ones, but those views of the scene were too far away.

"And the angles are all wrong." Duncan squinted to bring them into better focus. "Let's see something from the Western side of the street looking across to the church on the Eastern side." It came up and showed him walking out of the church yard, onto the sidewalk and then turning north towards the parked SUV that was also facing north.

"Enhance it… There," he pointed to the moment just before he leapt off the sidewalk into the street behind the SUV.

"Run second energy trail search, also spectral analysis and cross reference with the first," Monzo instructed.

"Completed."

"Yes!" Monzo did one of her trademark, old-school, James Brown slides, a few feet across the floor, her soft black curls bouncing on her shoulders as with both forefingers she pointed to the side-by-side red '98% and 100% Verndari' flashing on the case wall like a beacon in the night. "How yuh like me now?"

"Monzo, you're a damn genius." Dorran shook his head, looking stunned.

"True," she beamed.

"Seek and you shall find." Duncan gave her a solid pat on the shoulder.

Chapter 9

Proverbs 18:21
Death and life are in the power of the tongue: and they
that love it shall eat the fruit thereof...

"Finance. Good morning."

"Wow... What's good about that?"

"Detective?"

"You know, I didn't think it possible–" Detective Wright's deep voice, minus video, came through her air screen, "–but *that* was an even chillier reception than the one I got from you on that first day we met. And, after I just spent like ten minutes listening to hover-cab music, waiting on the line to get through to you, if I were a less secure man, I'd start to take it personally. What's the matter? Got those old Monday morning blues, Miz. Cole?" She could hear the smile in the tenor of his voice, and it was contagious.

"My humble apologies, Detective. And after you just saved my life? God forbid I should give you, of all people, anything less than a warm greeting." She grinned. "And no, I don't ever get the Monday blues. I'm just having some challenges with an employee this morning. Sorry, guess it came through in my voice. But not to worry, nothing I can't handle." She hoisted herself up in her chair.

"No doubt," he agreed.

Wondering why he'd waited so long on the office line, she flipped a few screens on her wristwatch, to see if she missed a call from him.

"Why didn't you just call my personal number though?"

"You know, I distinctly remember sharing *my* contact info with you at the theatre, but I don't seem to recall you reciprocating and giving me yours."

"Oh…? So, *Detective*–" she stressed on his title, "–is this the part where you pretend like you couldn't very easily find out what my digits are? Including everything from my social security number to my bra size?" She grinned as he barked out a laugh and started coughing.

"Oh my gosh, are you okay?" she giggled.

"Oh yeah, no, I'm good. That one made me choke on my coffee. Literally." His laughter rumbled up again. "You got me. That was…ah…unexpected…

"A lot like you, I'm learning."

Silence…

She slid the note-taker on her desk a few inches to the left, straightened it and curled her bare toes into the plush carpet under her desk. "So…what's up? How can I assist you today?"

He cleared his throat. "Well, I just thought I should see if you've had anything else unusual and/or unfortunate happen to you, since that fall yesterday."

"Oh no, believe it or not, I managed to make it all the way home and in to work today safe and sound. Without incident, thank God."

"Good. Glad to hear it."

"Actually, I forgot to ask yesterday. Any progress on Margot's case?" she wondered.

"Some."

"Anything you can share?"

"Not at this point, but I'll be in touch if there's anything you should know."

"Okay thanks, I'd appreciate that."

"Sure."

Silence reigned, again…

"Okay, so if there's nothing else…I've got to get back to it, but thanks so much for checking in, Detective."

"Yes, of course, think nothing of it. Just doing my job. I won't keep you any longer, well…except to say…and this is just a guess by the way…you're like what–a 32C?"

She gasped.

"You have a good one, Miz Cole," he rang off on a low chuckle.

Feeling her face heat, at the accuracy of his guess, she put a hand over her mouth to stifle a loud burst of laughter.

<hr>

Knock, knock.

What now?

Her buzz from her little engaging tête-à-tête with Detective Wright long since faded, Rissa found herself grappling with too much work and too tight a deadline when–

"Hey girl, why so quiet today?" Ally stood in her office doorway. "You didn't even come to the break room for birthday cake this afternoon." She entered. "Here you go. I saved you a slice.

"Chocolate cheesecake…" Ally's tone turned musical. "Your fa-vo-rite."

"Thanks Ally." She took a quick look as her friend deposited a gift of chocolate goodness on her desk and then went back to punching in numbers on her spreadsheet.

"So? What do you think?" Ally turned the shiny silver disk upon which the cake sat to the left and then to the right and a holo with a burst of colorful fireworks exploded in a perfect circle all around the cake, followed by a series of cute male models blowing happy birthday kisses in all directions.

"Joss absolutely loved it! She did that little shimmy-shimmy dance she does when she's excited, and I swear her face would have split in two if she'd grinned any wider.

"I've gotta say, you know I'm never one to be all supportive of HR's motivational agenda, but getting all the managers to take turns planning birthday celebrations for the line staff was just a stroke of genius. It really helps to foster genuine camaraderie and bring all members of the team together for more than just work. The staff love it! And it def shows in their performance."

"Mm-hmm." Rissa returned her attention to her spreadsheet.

"Hey, you okay? You don't think it's too much, do you, or inappropriate for the workplace?"

"Oh yeah, uh…no, it's fine. It's actually a great choice." She looked up and gave Ally an enthusiastic thumbs up. "It's exactly the kind of thing that would appeal to our young, boy-crazy intern."

With a wave of her hand, Rissa lifted and then shifted her virtual keypad to the right of her air-screen. She removed her glasses, rubbed her eyes, and leaned back in her chair.

"Don't mind me. I'm just having one of those

days where I'm finding it hard to keep my rules." She referred to her latest quest in her faith journey to not speak unless what she had to say met three critical criteria.

"Oh…" Ally nodded her understanding. "Which one? Truth?"

"Nope."

"Necessary?"

"Oh, it's necessary all right," she paused, as she considered the disciplinary discussion she absolutely needed to have with a particularly difficult and insubordinate non-performer.

"Okay…so kind, then."

"Bingo! Yatzee! Ding! Ding! Ding! Tell her what she's won Johnny!"

Ally clapped a hand to her mouth and looked to the open door as she let out a loud burst of laughter. "How do you come up with those odd sayings?"

"Entirely too much 21st century TV." She shook her head as she recalled hearing it on an old Jim Carrey movie she'd enjoyed just the week before.

"Now go. Save yourself!" she sang as she waved her friend to the door with a grin.

"Okay, I'll see you later hon." Still laughing, Ally quit the room.

Rissa sighed, put her glasses back on and refreshed her air-screen with a wave of her hand. Through the lighter spots in the spreadsheet, she could still see the cake. Reaching out she pulled it around to the side, raised the tiny fork and cut a small bite off a corner.

She took a taste.

"Damn Hunter…" under her breath she addressed the latest popular male heartthrob to blow a kiss at her as she licked the dessert fork "…that's some good cake. *Really* good choice, Ally."

She pulled it towards her and dug in with relish.

Chapter 10

Romans 16:18
For they that are such serve not our Lord Jesus Christ,
but their own belly; and by good words and fair
speeches deceive the hearts of the simple ...

Well, thanks to her non-performer it was 8.15pm, and Rissa was still hard at work at her desk. Everyone had long since gone home, even the cleaners on her floor had said goodnight to her at least an hour earlier. She figured she just needed another half hour, and she'd be finished.

Wait…What was that…?

She looked to her office doorway as she heard the whisper of a strange voice.

"Hello?" she called out. But there was no

answer. Odd, she was sure she'd heard something. She turned back to her work.

Wait, there it was again.

Rising from her desk this time, she didn't put on her shoes but walked quickly to her doorway on bare feet. She was in a large corner office, so she looked to the right. It was a fair distance to the cubicles that housed her Finance division, but then closer to her entryway she noticed a strange greyish haze moving around the carpet a couple feet away.

What in the world? Is that smoke?

She took a step back and before she could react, the shadowy haze rushed in, swirled around and then surrounded her. Her head spun as it lifted her high, almost to the ceiling.

"N-n-no! No-ooo!" Her protest ended on her blood curdling scream, as she was flung with incredible force, across the room towards the glass wall of her fifth story office.

"Oh!" she gasped, and her eyes snapped open, as someone caught her in strong arms.

Just like Lois Lane with her Superman, she clung to her hero's neck as he glided back down to earth. She stared, into striking, bright, sky-blue eyes. Saw such warmth, in his familiar face.

"Hey Rissa." He grinned, as he lowered her feet gently to the floor.

"Oh, my gosh…I remember you."

Here was the man of her dreams, literally, who'd

just recently urged her to pray after one of the most disturbing experiences of her life. Standing in her office as real as could be. "Who…how…?" She looked around as she released his neck, trying to figure out where he'd come from and where the dark force that had just tried to end her life had gone.

Oh God, have mercy…

Maybe it was him! After all, he was there when she'd been thrown out of that strange tunnel.

She started to back away.

"Satan cannot cast out Satan," his voice resonated with quiet strength and godly wisdom, "and if he rise up against himself and be divided, he cannot stand."

She stopped her retreat. Recognized the scriptural significance of his words, but she was still afraid. "Is that what that was? Some kind of evil spirit?"

He nodded.

"And you?"

"Your guardian angel."

He said the words, and just like that, she saw a revelation of the immense blessing he had been in her life, up to that point, in overwhelming flashes in her mind. And from the sheer intensity of it and the associated feelings, she sensed another scream bubbling up.

"Okay now, before you panic, I need you to just hear me out," he held up a cajoling hand, "please.

"Let's see…your middle name is Catherine; you like a sprinkling of crushed almonds and slices of sweet berries on your 'death by chocolate' cake, your favorite hymn is "Great is thy Faithfulness," and you've been terrified of thunderstorms for as long as you can remember."

"Just the lightning, not the thunder," they said in unison.

"Oh, and I wouldn't sit there if I were you," he pointed, as weak in the knees she was lowering herself into the closest chair around the conference table. "That's the one with the busted wheel."

She delayed her descent, shifted to the left and then sat down.

"Okay, so now you're just showing off."

"Not even a remote possibility when you've seen what I have." He smiled and walked over from where they'd landed near the glass wall.

"Hi. I'm Alcindor–" He raised his right palm and placed it over the left side of his chest, "–and I've been watching over you for a very long time, Alrissa Catherine Cole." He extended the hand. "It's a rare pleasure to actually meet you."

Sure…why not?

Hell, after the month she'd had - three near-death experiences and one near-mauling by a jungle cat, she was ready to believe just about anything. Plus of course, he'd literally just appeared out of nowhere and caught her in mid-air, AKA near-death experience number three. No biggie.

Whether disarmed by his charming manner, winning smile, and persuasive words–

And who wouldn't trust that face?

–against all logic, she took his outstretched hand.

Whoa...

Touching his hand felt like Christmas morning when she was six, holding Sam on the day he was born and that very first, big bite of her favorite chocolate cheesecake... mmm... All rolled into one.

In a word... Joy.

She released his hand and clenched both of hers into fists on the table in front of her, to stop herself from reaching out for the drug that was him.

"Sorry. Too much?"

"Huh?"

"The bliss. I dialed it down for you, but sometimes I don't filter like I should."

"Yeah, I can relate," she shook her head on a chuckle.

"Yeah, I know," he smiled.

A smile that was just so adorable. She had this urge. He made her want to just reach up and hug him, repeatedly. "Please...take a seat." She remembered her manners.

"Thank you." He sat in the chair right across the table from hers.

"Wow." She lost her fear but was still stunned.

"I always thought guardian angels being here on earth was a made-up story adults told children to make them feel safe and protected."

"Oh, we're very real. Aside from normal life, all throughout history, in every century, we're at every miraculous event – acting, or inspiring humans to act. Every time only a single person survived a plane crash, or when those heroic firemen saved so many during the attacks of 9/11, in the early 21st century. Scientists, who amplified the force field technology that saved millions of people in New Atlantis when the domes started to crack in Jan 2120. A few of them were Guardians."

"To God be the glory," they both said and shared a smile.

"I know this is a whole lot for you to take in and ordinarily you'd never even know we're around, but these are perilous times for you." He lost his smile. "You've only seen a small glimpse of spiritual evil, on your night travels."

"A small glimpse?"

He nodded.

Rissa considered her many terrifying late-night encounters and was ready to contradict his suggestion that there was much she hadn't seen. Until…

"It's far worse than you could ever imagine, Rissa. I don't mean to frighten you, but if you could see with your inward eyes to the spiritual plane that exists within this physical one, you'd see clusters of demons literally clinging onto the bodies of the lost and weak-minded. They're all around, ceaselessly spreading their evil, fear, hate, and avarice."

She felt her blood run cold at the horrific picture he painted.

"Well, it's a good thing you didn't want to scare me Al. Next time you might wanna try harder," she gave a half laugh. "Seriously though, are any of them here…now?" She brushed her hands over her forearms, feeling chilled.

"No," he shook his head. "I and my fellow messengers serve the one true God – Father, Creator, Spirit. We carry and reflect His light." His smile was heart-stopping. "The fallen cannot exist within, or around it, unless we conceal it, or the Creator allows them."

Rissa was relieved and immensely moved by his words and the wonder of his joy-filled expression.

"Your enemy is–"

"Your enemy?" she interrupted. "We're in this thing together my friend. Don't you mean 'our'?"

"No, Rissa, the battle is with men alone. It is finished and settled in heavenly places."

"Okay, bear with me," she held up her hands, "I understand that, in the context of the price paid for our salvation, but what about the end of times. The good news of the kingdom shall be preached in all the world for a witness unto all nations; and then the end will come." She quoted from the good book. He nodded. "Well then, don't you also have a fight on your doorstep until every single person on the planet hears the Word?"

"Hundreds of thousands of children are born around the world every day. There is no final day of mankind. Instead, as more and more receive the Word and pass it on through generations, on the very day that such becomes the way without exception, the day that only the Father knows, it is then that men will usher in the return of the Son of Man.

"Satan was vanquished at the cross, yet you humans continue to revive him over and over again.

"He lives…only in you."

The impact of that simple truth hit her like a sucker-punch to the gut.

She felt rare tears spring to her eyes. They were the worst kinds of fools indeed–ones who orchestrated their own demise and then danced amongst the ashes.

"And you won't want to hear this next bit either."

She felt her heart sink.

"But, given all that's happened, even as you ramp up your prayer life, you also need to be on your guard…I'm afraid there's more to Verndari than they're saying. They aren't really aliens from another planet. They're actually kinda like me."

"Huh…? They're angels too?"

"Yes, and no." He stood, paced away and then returned to stand before her. "They are the one third. They're exiles–the fallen ones. The angels who joined with evil eons ago and were cast out. Down here. To earth."

"What?!"

She absorbed the meaning in his words and intent look, even as her mind rebelled against the notion. "No way!" She made a rude sound.

"Oh, yes way," Al nodded.

"Demons?"

He nodded again.

"Oh my gosh..."

A recent survey had estimated the ratio of defenders to humans on earth was nearly one for every two.

"You've got to be kidding me." Rissa bent her forehead into her upturned hands as she considered the magnitude of this latest revelation.

She knew being of God he couldn't, didn't lie, so maybe he was just mistaken?

"But that just doesn't make sense. Wait. Just hear me out for a minute." She held up the forefingers of both hands as she looked up at him. "Just look at how much they've done for us since they revealed themselves. Demons would never help us. There have been almost immediate cures for major diseases like cancer and–"

"That only rich folk can afford, so greedy Big

Pharma can continue to line their already fat pockets." He interjected with a stoic tone before she could even give voice to her full thought.

"Oh Kayyy…" Reluctant, she acknowledged that truth and searched her mind for the next grand development she was sure had accompanied the arrival of the defenders.

"Oh, oh!" she snapped her fingers. "All those new technological advances. Like–"

"Mostly revamped tech with unpublicized applications for new and more powerful weapons. So basically, bigger and better ways for you guys to damn your souls as you kill each other." He dropped back into his chair directly opposite hers and pushed away from the table as he crossed a booted foot over his knee.

"Really?"

"'Fraid so," he nodded.

"Oh, come on. Give me a break here," she breathed as she rubbed her forehead for inspiration.

"Okay, so what about the new food supply. They've put one of those fantastic never-ending food dispensers in nearly every populated area across the globe, so people can eat for free." She rose from her seat and walked around the table.

"You absolutely cannot find some nefarious agenda in," she quoted the now popular and very accurate slogan with a curved hand in the air to punctuate each word.

"'Hunger. No. More.'"

"Oh yeah, you mean all the junk food and artificial sweets, right?" He swung his chair around to face her. "Can you say –" He mimicked her hand gesture, "Obesity. Heart disease. Childhood diabetes?

"Look up the stats, Rissa. They've cut the average human's lifespan by twenty years with those machines."

"But the dozens of ships they came in…" She felt a cloud of confusion surrounding her. "Video of their arrival across the world was everywhere. All over mainstream news and social media for months."

"Parlor tricks. Think about it. Have you ever seen one of those so-called ships since? Has anyone? That's because they never actually landed. They just appeared in the night sky, delivered up their occupants and then vanished. Mere illusions, to make men believe the biggest lie in history. And you made it easy for them. Thanks to mankind's fascination and desire to find life on other planets, you literally opened your doors wide for them to walk right in."

Rissa was stunned.

Lying signs and wonders…

"Face it. They've come to kill, steal, and destroy just like their leader. Physically and spiritually, they're corrupting as many as they can, as fast as they can.

"And one more thing you need to know. On the

odd occasion we must materialize to save a soul…how can I explain this…we blend in with our surroundings to meet a need or a threat, so we take different forms. We can imitate your speech patterns and adopt the colloquialisms of the day. Basically, become anyone at any time."

"What about animals?"

"Yes, animals as well."

"So that was you…the wolf in my tent last week?"

He nodded.

"And the panther?"

"A fallen one who has tried to separate himself from Legion. He has acquired a taste for murder, so you must be vigilant."

"So, he's the one killing women in the area?"

"Yes."

She felt ill, as another thought struck "And Margot?"

He nodded, just once.

"So why don't you just, you know–?" she made a slicing gesture with a finger against her throat.

"Not his time and not my call."

"So, basically what you're saying is, I have to be on the look-out for a shape-shifting, serial-killing, defender-demon." Her intended question came out as more of a horrified statement.

"Oh…

"…Crap," she breathed. She dropped back into

her seat and hung her head as the significance of it all took alarming root in her mind.

"Yeah, it pretty much sucks. Well…for you."

Startled, she looked up.

"No? Too much?"

"Seriously?" She sighed. "We're talking *epic* filter-failure."

"Really? Cause the way your candor and sense of humor are sort of spliced together, I thought for sure that would be funny, right about, ah…now…" his voice trailed off, his look sheepish as she shook her head at him.

"No Al. Like now, now would be a really good time to dial back the slang and the attempts to lighten the mood there, buddy." She made a backward circular motion with her forefingers. "Not the time and def not helping."

She sighed again.

Chapter 11

Psalms 16:11
Thou wilt shew me the path of life: in thy presence is
fulness of joy; at thy right hand there are pleasures for
evermore…

Al walked Rissa out to her car.

"Are you sure you're, okay? Because I could go with you, if you'd like. Well…I'm always with you, but I could stay on this plane of existence, visible to you, so you'll *see* that I'm with you." He gestured with a hand. "You know what I mean."

She nodded her understanding. "No need. I'm fine." She straightened her blazer, squared her shoulders, then looked over at him. Gave him a reassuring smile and held his gaze, as she stepped forward near the bonnet of her car.

"Woah, easy there," he grasped her arm and waist to steady her, just as she missed her footing and slipped on the edge of the pavement. Feeling her foot slide out from under her, she thought she narrowly missed falling into the water-filled gutter between her car and another that was parked nearby.

"On second thought–" his lips quirked upward, as he raised a hand to his mouth and coughed, "–you know what? That was actually quite a scare you had back there." He turned a bit to the side, facing away from her. "Maybe I should just go with you." He glanced up at the sky. "If for nothing more than…ah–" he coughed again, "–you know, moral support," his voice sounded strangled at the last.

"Just look at you. You wanna laugh so much, you can't even look me in the eye, can you?" She grasped his arm and pulled him around to face her, then put her hands on her hips as she glared at him.

His lips twitched again, he smiled, grinned, and then burst into loud laughter.

"I'm sorry," he waved a hand in the air, then put the thumb of a closed fist to his mouth as he continued laughing, "but you should have seen the look on your face. It was just priceless!"

"Yeah, Ha-Ha. Laugh it up Al." She dusted imaginary dirt off her trouser leg "Some guardian you are. I could have busted my skull open. How would you know?"

"Actually, I *do* know," his laughter faded and he smiled. "And the worst you would have been looking at, is a bruised ego. Once your butt hit the pavement, and your shoe flew up in the air, leaving you with your bare left foot in the water, and your right hand in something that trust me, you do not wanna hear about." He shook his head from side to side.

She stared at him, in silence, for a few seconds.

"Really?" Then gave him a look, intended to wither.

He shrugged. "You asked."

She shook her head.

"Here, allow me." He opened her car door for her, and then held out an open hand.

"Sure, why not." She took it. "Especially since I've apparently now lost the ability to walk on my own." He gave a wry chuckle, as he gallantly helped her into her car.

"Need me to drive?" he bent over and grinned, as he looked in at her through the open window.

"Just get in." She turned to start the car as she heard the return of his laughter. "I already feel like enough of an idiot, without compounding it by letting you add chauffeuring duties to your no doubt impressive resume."

He chuckled as he came around to the other side, and dropped into the front passenger seat.

"Where'd you even learn to drive, anyway? Don't you fly everywhere in heaven." She smirked at him.

"And just like that guy says in that sitcom you watch all the time–don't be such a hate–err," he turned a serious look on her and dropped his voice an octave. "It's so *not* a good look on you."

She regarded him for a bit, then they both burst into loud laughter. They were still laughing, as she pulled the car away from the curb and headed for home.

"God loves a good laugh, doesn't He?" she wondered, after their amusement faded. She hit the auto-driver button and turned to face him.

"Do you?"

She met his gaze. Caught his serious expression.

"Well, yeah. Of course." She raised a hand and gestured with an open palm.

"You are made in His glorious image, Rissa–

"–You bet He does."

She nodded, comforted, as they shared a secret smile.

———•●•———

"So, I think I have enough left of my famous lasagna, for two." She ushered him into her home nearly a half hour later. "Can I offer you something to eat, or to drink?"

"You could, but I wouldn't enjoy it." He dropped down onto her sofa, his tone, matter of fact.

"What did you just say?" Hers, was sharp.

His head jerked up.

"Oh, I'm so sorry Rissa. Filter-failure. That didn't come out right. I just meant that what I'm used to is…different. The kingdom is not about food and drink; but righteousness and peace and joy in the Holy Spirit." His smile was brilliant, as he quoted from the good book. "The pleasures of heaven–" the arc he made with his hands was expansive, "–are beyond anything that you could ever imagine. And not in and of themselves, but solely because at their very core, at an intrinsic level that you cannot yet comprehend, is always the communion and the fellowship with the Three in One."

"Wow…" she felt more than a twinge of envy.

"It's a powerful thing. You have no idea," he beamed. "So, even though we won't share a meal, we can certainly pray together and read the Word if you'd like?" He pointed to the leather-bound bible she had sitting on the edge of her coffee table, where she'd left it the night before. It was a recent gift from Ally. A treasured rarity, given the proliferation of electronic readers in her century. There was just something so comforting about the feel of turning the paper pages with her fingers. She felt closer somehow, to the hundreds of generations of the faithful, who had done so before her.

"I think it will really help you, as you go through this next phase of your journey."

"Pray," she nodded. "Right… You know, in my mind's eye, I can still see your big cardboard sign. Now, *that* was inspired."

"Got your attention, didn't it?" he grinned.

"Oh, yes. That it did. So, yes. I would love that. Thank you so much.

"This is so nice, isn't it?" she smiled across at him. "I mean, you'd know this, obviously. But so far, I haven't really been able to find someone who shares my interests, like my crazy love of 21st Century tv," she sang as she wiggled her fingers in the air, then tucked a few strands of hair behind her ear, wondering how best to engage him further.

He gave her a curious look.

"You know that nothing more than this–" he leaned forward made a steeple with his fingers over the bible, "–can happen between us, right?" He leaned back again and peered at her.

"Oh yeah, of course, of course." She waved a dismissive hand in the air.

"Okay. I know you've had a rough night. So, we can start tomorrow, when you get in from work?"

She nodded.

"Which book would you like us to cover first?"

Well, uh…" she tried to shake off her disappointment at his mild rejection, "…we're doing Job in bible study at the moment, so getting your perspective on it would be phenomenal."

"Excellent choice." He smiled. "I'll see you, or

rather…you'll see me, tomorrow then." He grinned. "Goodnight, Rissa. Stay blessed."

He disappeared, before she could even return the farewell.

Chapter 12

1 Peter 5:8
Be sober, be vigilant; because your adversary the devil,
as a roaring lion, walketh about, seeking whom he may
devour…

Alrissa had a mostly sleepless night, no doubt all courtesy of Guardian Al's little revelation about the alien demons.

Or maybe it was demon aliens…

Her mind was still spinning, long after he disappeared from her home, as quickly as he'd appeared in her office. And it only got worse from there, since, by the end of the following three weeks, her nerves were well and truly frayed to the breaking point.

There had been two more attempts on her life, that she knew of, since those were in the natural. Al saved her again, both times and in spectacular fashion. He even mentioned something about having to also thwart attacks in the spirit realm and when he wouldn't elaborate, she figured she was better off not knowing.

He was her champion, her prayer warrior, and her best friend. The literal man of her dreams who knew her even better than she knew herself. Warm, kind, selfless, with a great sense of humor. Everything she'd ever prayed to have in a companion.

It was a good thing his angel code kept him from reading her mind. He'd explained that while he certainly had the capability and always had a connection to her, he stopped short of the invasion of privacy that following her thoughts would be.

A good thing indeed, since it was def time to face it.

She was falling for her angel.

And going straight to hell, obviously. She slapped an open palm to her forehead.

Do not pass go. Do not collect $200.

Thank God for her work. Her fortress of solitude, where everything just made sense. It was mid-morning, and she breathed a sigh of relief as she sat at her desk in front of a particularly complicated discounted cashflow, and considered the wonderful comfort she found in the precision of financial accounting. Every dollar in its place, every debit had its equal and corresponding credit, every–

"You know, you need to be extra careful given Helen's death today, Rissa."

She jumped and pushed her chair back, then jerked her head forward to avoid hitting it against the wall. "Really Al?" She looked to where he was comfortably seated on her visitor's couch. "A little warning next time? You scared the heck out of me!"

"Oh yeah, sorry about the sore neck." He winced and pointed.

And, she started to rub it, as a crick almost immediately manifested right at the base of her skull. Familiar as she now was, with his clairvoyance for whenever she was in pain or danger, she didn't even bother to comment.

"Geez, who knew being under angel-watch would come with this many occupational hazards. If you were human I swear, you'd need Professional Indemnity insurance, yeah, that's what you should get," she groaned. He grinned.

"Here, let me." He disappeared from the couch, appeared at her back, and began to rub out not just the pain in her neck, but also the knots of near-permanent tension in her shoulders.

"Is that better?"

Her heart skipped a beat.

Oh...my glorious heaven...

It was like she could hear the hallelujah chorus.

"Knock, knock." The words accompanied a double tap on her office door jamb. "Good afternoon Miz. Cole. I was hoping I could have a few minutes of your time regarding the death of someone from the fourth floor."

She jumped up, dislodging Al's hands from her shoulders with her rapid rise. "Detective? Hi! Sure, come on in."

He took a few steps forward and glanced around. Looking rugged-casual, his muscled legs were encased in slim fitting blue jeans, and he'd topped off the look with a gray shirt and a navy accented blazer.

"Ah..." she moved to the side of her desk, closest to where he'd entered, looked back at Al, and extended an open hand in his direction. "Let me introduce you to–"

Old friend? Kissing cousin?

Self Defense Coach! That was kind of true, wasn't it?

"He can't see, or hear me, unless I want him to Rissa." Al spoke close to her ear, just as she decided on option number three.

He walked around her and stood directly in front of Detective Wright. He waved. "See? Nothing."

"Oh Okay. Ah...yes, let me introduce you to my...ah...world," she hit on an acceptable alternative and smiled as she extended her other hand as well, in a sweeping arc, to encompass her office.

Al laughed out loud.

"Oh, now *this* should be real entertaining to watch." He grinned as he walked around the front of her desk and retook his seat on the sofa.

She glared at him then turned back to her guest.

Detective Wright also looked towards the sofa.

"So, this is where all the magic happens–" she redirected his attention to her desk, "– and of course outside in my division. I couldn't do this without them, after all." She pumped her fist. "Go Team!"

She heard a chuckle or two from the couch but refused to look.

"Magic, huh?" The left side of his mouth lifted. "And what does magic look like to you, Miz Cole?"

"Hmm…let's see…" She held her chin and tapped a finger on her cheek. "Maybe a Balance Sheet?"

"How so?"

"Well, it's like a perfect union of two people, where the positive attributes, AKA the assets of one, effectively balance with and cancel out the liabilities of the other."

"So, you're speaking from experience?" He looked amused.

Al disappeared off the couch and appeared again in front of Detective Wright. "Is it just me, or are you two getting just a tad bit personal?" He tiptoed up to the detective's height and looked right into his face.

"Maybe I should leave?"

"No, I'm not, and you should." She answered both of Al's questions.

"Really? Me? I should speak from *my* experience?" Detective Wright's half smile and deep, rumbling laugh held untold possibilities. "What makes you say that?"

"Okay then. Later." Al popped out.

She gestured to one of the two seats in front of her desk, as she sat behind it. "You should…sit down Detective, is what I was going to say."

"No, you weren't, you little fibber-fish." Al popped back into the same spot, with a huge, silly grin on his adorable face–

"But hey, great save!" –and a thumbs up.

She resisted the urge to wince over the untruth *and* throw her note-taker at him.

"Okay. I'm out. For real this time."

"Okay." Automatically, she raised a hand to wave and had to run it over her hair instead.

Al disappeared in a fit of laughter.

She took a cleansing breath.

"So, Detective, what's this about another death?"

He shook his head, his attractive lips lifting in a slight smile, as he took the seat she indicated and flipped open his notepad. "Yes, Helen Camden. One of the security guards found her this morning when he opened the supply closet on the ground floor."

She felt sick all over again, just like when she'd heard the awful news, through the office grapevine, when she arrived that morning. Helen was one of the other 'lucky' winners of a ticket to the Awards and now she'd met her maker far too soon, just like Margot.

"So how well did you know this deceased?"

"Not very. She was the head of PR, so I had about the same contact with her that I had with Margot."

"Did you see her at the Awards?"

It felt like déjà vu as he began his rapid-fire line of questioning.

"No, I looked for her in the lobby, but there were so many people milling around, by the time the show got started I'd only seen Margot and Terri."

"What about after? Did she mention meeting anyone special, like maybe *your* GQ-holo defender?" His lips compressed into a tight line.

"No, she didn't mention meeting anyone and not that it's any of your business, but he isn't *my* anything Detective. I just met him the one time, and we barely spoke."

Okay, so maybe not déjà vu, since their delightful tit for tat was sadly absent this time, instead, the tension between them felt weird and uncomfortable.

"And based on the little you knew about Ms. Camden; did she and Ms. Channing have any habits, or hobbies in common? Could be as innocuous as working out at the same fitness center."

"I don't know. I can't recall them discussing any shared interests," she sighed and slumped in her chair, as she felt her angel-massage buzz evaporate.

"And what about you?" He gave her a sharp look. "What did you have in common with them?"

"Me?" she squeaked and pulled herself up in a quick jerk. "What do I have to do with any of this?"

"Two women are dead, Miz. Cole. Under suspicious circumstances. And like you, they both worked out of this firm, and again, like you, they both attended that award ceremony." He leaned forward and held her gaze in his intense one. "These… threats, they seem to be happening around you, and I don't like it…" he shifted a bit in his chair, "… maybe we haven't made the connection yet, but I don't believe in coincidences. You need to be extra careful given Ms. Camden's death today. This unsub is escalating, and I've got a very bad feeling in my gut, that you're a target too."

"Oh, come on, there's no evidence of that." She dismissed his assertion with a wave of her hand. If there was one thing she'd learned about Detective Wright, it was that he was sharp as a tack. Afraid she was being very expertly maneuvered into a place where an alien-demon revelation would be her only viable response, swiftly followed by a long stay in a mental institution, she doubled down.

"Don't you worry about me detective. I'm blessed, plus I carry a can of pepper spray in my purse, and I know how to use it," she nodded. "I'm perfectly safe…I'm even thinking about taking some self-defense sessions. I've always wanted to do something like that. I really enjoyed the karate classes I took when I was a kid. True, I didn't make it all the way to black belt, but I was…Detective…?"

He was staring. In the direction of her office's massive glass wall.

"Perfectly safe huh?" He pointed to it and she turned.

There in big, bold letters, as though someone had breathed on the glass and then written in the condensation were the words–

YOU'RE NEXT

Oh…crap…

———•●•———

Frustrated, Duncan headed back to the precinct. The literal writing on the wall disappeared without a trace, a second after it appeared, but he knew she'd seen it. Her expression–one of raw fear, told him as much. Of course, she denied it, but it didn't matter, because he knew what he'd seen. And aside from the message, he'd seen a woman in known peril.

It was there, in the faint bluish circles under her pretty brown eyes and in hair that was just a bit disheveled, though still arousing as all hell to him. Like she'd just climbed out of his bed…

He shook his head and groaned–the sound–more like a growl.

Ordinarily she was so well put together - a knock-out brunette in a business suit.

He grinned.

Damn. For someone so beautiful, intelligent, and oh-so-sexy, she sure was stubborn as a mule. He'd tried to get her to take a protective detail, but she flatly refused. He'd still arranged for someone to watch her home, and he'd tap into the traffic cam footage outside her office building just in case.

"Hey Monzo."

She was back at the case wall, hard at work when he walked into the squad room.

"Okay, so we already know the aliens are in this up to their eyeballs." She turned from the wall and acknowledged his greeting with a nod as he hung his blazer over the back of his chair. "So, I say we go old school on their butts. Motive, means, and opportunity." She ticked off each one on a different finger. "I never trusted all that "we come in peace" bull crap." Her face was a mask of anger. "It's the strangest thing…can't say why, but I've just had this feeling they have a world domination agenda. But what do they stand to gain by killing all these women? How does it further that agenda?"

"Beats me." Duncan shrugged and leaned back

in his chair. "Other than the two from the media house, none of the others have any connection. They have completely different lifestyles and interests. My guess? They're just a bunch of rando strangers who, maybe, found themselves in the wrong place, at an even worse time."

"Maybe." She shrugged. "Now the means I get," she pointed to their notes on the wall. "It's clearly some kinda next-level, freaky invisibility tech. Plus, they're strong as hell. Pretty sure I saw one lift a car once, tossed it aside like it was nothing, so they could def shatter some poor woman's neck."

"What?!" Duncan felt icy dread ripple down his spine as he leaned forward. "And you're just sharing this bit of info now?"

"It was years ago." She turned from the wall, dismissed his alarm with a casual wave of a hand. "Plus, at the time, I wasn't sure myself if I'd maybe just imagined the whole episode," she shrugged. "But now, with everything that's been happening, and since this morning, it's all been coming back to me, real clear… like a shooting star… across the dark night sky."

She paused. And got a faraway look in her eyes.

"Uh…where was I–" she shook her head, "–oh yeah–their most recent opportunity. Now *that* we know, cause a couple of them made a rare appearance at the Awards show. So, I say we start there. Get a guest list and see what's poppin'."

"Yeah, and let's start with the one called–" Duncan grabbed his notepad and flipped backwards a couple dozen pages, "–Svikari. He was there that night, and a few people said he's in PR and wouldn't you know it, so is today's vic. It's like I always say Monzo, I don't believe in coincidences." She pointed a forefinger at him in agreement as she headed to the door. "So, what are we waiting for? Grab your jacket and let's go get this son of a..." her voice trailed off as she disappeared through it.

He shrugged it on and hastened to follow.

Chapter 13

1 Corinthians 2:9
But as it is written, eye hath not seen, nor ear heard,
neither have entered into the heart of man, the things
which God hath prepared for them that love him…

Well, of the string of terrible times she'd been having of late, this one sure took the cake.

And she wasn't just thinking about the uncomfortable night she spent tossing and turning in bed, after receiving her own personal 'get ready for your imminent death' message.

The next morning, Rissa gave a vigorous shake of her head, from left to right, as though by doing, so she could somehow break free from the lingering images of leering, hideously twisted faces as she flew backwards, keeping them all in view as she tried her best to dodge the sting of tiny needles aimed right at her.

Oh joy. Now they're using me for target practice.

She grabbed a coffee from the break room and hustled to her office to get her day started.

Sometime after dawn, she'd been roaming again, around strange places and amid even stranger beings that kept chasing her. So now she was late for work and exhausted.

"Another bad night? Oh Rissa…" Over the top of her coffee mug, she spied the pity in her friend's expression as she rapped on her doorjamb, walked in, and plopped down on the plush seating against the far wall.

More than a little uncomfortable, Rissa patted her hair into place and was left wondering whether she looked that bad, or–*Oh no*…had she become guilty of the dreaded 'over-share'? She didn't know which scenario held less appeal.

"No, no." She placed her favorite 'Faith' mug on her desk, waved away Ally's concern and put on her brightest smile. "Last night wasn't that bad. Truly," she added when Ally's look remained unchanged.

"I actually only remember a moment." She fought the urge to cringe, as she broke her 'truth' rule. "I was out soaring through the air again and the weirdest looking bird flew alongside me for a bit. It was misshapen, like somebody tried to merge a pterodactyl with a caricature of a parrot, I guess. I mean just butt-ugly, with bulging eyes, all rough edges, and pointy angles." She pointed to her friend's expression as Ally made a face. "Yes, my thought exactly. I remember wondering what in the world I was looking at."

"Another one of those evil minions in disguise probably."

"No…this was different."

"From everything you've said, how can you tell?"

"Easy," she shrugged. "It didn't try to kill me."

"Wow." Ally's eyes were wide as she put a hand to her throat.

"Plus, just before it flew away, I had this word in my spirit, that our great Creator's work is singular, unmatchable, so the devil can only pervert his creations. It's like no matter how hard he tries he could never make anything original, or beautiful and it just fuels his hate, anger, and resentment."

"Wow, that's so real. We should def mention that during bible study."

"Sure, we could do that. Come to think of it. We're supposed to be doing some chapters from Genesis next, so that will be a great discussion point."

"Exactly." Ally pointed an index finger in her direction.

"Which also reminds me," Rissa grabbed the note-taker off her desk, waved a hand to close her door and hit the electro-privacy screen button on her desk on her way back. As a shimmer of grey came down along the door and the two inner walls of the room, she sat next to her friend. "I've been working on something for my presentation for the book of Revelation next week and I'd love it if you could weigh in and tell me what you think?"

"Sure, anything I can do to help."

"Great!" She pulled open the device, set it to play, placed the thimble-like receiver on her forefinger and launched right in.

"So, question–have you ever thought about forever? Every now and again I'm blessed with a moment, just a moment when in the Spirit I can feel what it's going to be like to be in heaven."

As she spoke, the unit on her lap lit with vivid hues. Images of beautiful vistas expanded outward from it, filling the room, as the resident AI interpreted her thoughts and feelings into moving pictures.

"I feel peace. I feel pure joy. Just a whisper and then it's gone again. Swallowed up and drowned out by this sinful world we live in." Dark images surged upward to the ceiling and flew all around them. Different from the first ones. This time they were of depravity, greed, and war.

"Our time on this planet is linear. We constantly move along a line from point A to point B, from morning to night–" the letters AM popped up at the top left of a floating screen that appeared directly in front of them and then a horizontal line crawled along from left to right to the letters PM, "–from day to day," directly below that line '1st'appeared and then another line slid over to '31st'. "–and from year to year." The year 2120 appeared and yet another line glided to where 2130 waited on the right.

"So, in essence, we're always just trudging along at some stage on the same lines, decade after decade, just waiting for the end of our particular line." Images of death and funerals with sorrowing families replaced the lines, filling the room and then faded just as quickly.

"But God's time isn't like that. Father God made time, so He's completely outside of it. So, what if in heaven, instead of being somewhere between the beginning and the end of a line, we're in the middle of a never-ending circle. With no beginning and no end."

A large, perfect sphere appeared with a single dot at its very center that grew and grew until it exploded into a rainbow of colors that filled the entire room with flashes of all the most beautiful scenes one could ever imagine–of smiling people, frolicking like children in joy and complete abandon on pristine, green landscapes, arrayed with a variety of colorful flowers, by a river of flowing crystal-clear water.

"Imagine it. No yesterday. No tomorrow. It's always just today. It's always now, as we literally forever live in a truly miraculous moment. Surrounded by love. Of our families, our friends. Connection, yes. But with no history, because He makes all things new." Like a flash of lightning, a bright beam shot out of the unit, outshining all the images until the entire room was awash in warm white light, pulsing in synch with the sound of a beating heart.

Thump-thump…thump-thump…

"Life on earth is so short, and yet we still find it too difficult to hold onto the fleeting and scarce moments that make it all worthwhile."

Thump-thump…thump-thump…

She closed her eyes. Inhaled deep as she prepared to deliver her last line.

"So wouldn't it be ironic, if when we finally have forever…is when we'll finally…finally be able to truly live in and savor, a single moment."

Thump.

Silence…

And light… So much light…

Hearing a loud sniff, Rissa's eyes popped open.

"Wow. That was amazing." Ally wiped tears from her cheeks with the back of her hand.

"Really? You liked it? It wasn't too out there?"

"No, not at all." She gave a vigorous shake of her head. "It was so beautiful and so thought provoking too. I never ever considered time could work that way. Wow…and the imagery. You missed your calling–you're an artist, girl."

"Who me? Nooo." Rissa looked down; a bit uncomfortable with the praise. "That's just the AI doing its thing."

"Oh, I don't think so. The tech is an excellent tool for sure, but it can only interpret thoughts and feelings. So that," she pointed to the unit on Rissa's lap, "that's ALL you, my friend!" She held up her hand for a high five. They did an imaginary clap in the air with hands that didn't meet as was their custom.

"Thanks so much Ally." They shared a grin.

"Now come on, we gotta go." Ally straightened her pretty, floral skirt as she rose and headed to the door. "We've got this month's alien sensitivity refresher in the conference room in five. That's why I came in here actually…to remind you." She looked back briefly as Rissa released the privacy control so she could open it.

"Oh, no, was that today? But I have a ton of work to do," Rissa grumbled as she looked at her watch, then closed the note-taker and placed it back on her desk.

Privately she considered the sheer futility of such instruction, given what she now knew about their alien friends.

We need to make them feel welcome and as

comfortable as possible, to encourage them to interact with us more. Learn to be empathetic, patient, and considerate whenever you have an opportunity to address a defender. Remember, they're probably still trying to learn our ways and habits...

The instructions of the facilitator from the last session echoed in her mind.

HA! Guaranteed they know us even better than we know ourselves.

They were likely just laying a trap with their anti-social behavior. Pretending to feel alienated so humans would bend over backwards to welcome them into their lives. Men would think the progressive assimilation was their idea and not recognize they'd been expertly manipulated instead. She stifled a snort.

"Maybe I could miss it?" she wondered aloud and sat down behind her desk.

"What? And incur the wrath of the entire HR division? Nooo. Trust me. You do not wanna do that." Ally's words trailed away as she disappeared out the door.

Rissa pictured a recent reprimand she'd received for the most trivial of supposed infractions. Soft elevator music playing in the background, at complete odds with the politically correct bashing being dispensed, all while she sat in one of their sterile 'safe-space' rooms...

"Good point." She jumped to her feet and hastened to follow Ally through the door.

Chapter 14

Matthew 10:28
And fear not them which kill the body, but are not able
to kill the soul: but rather fear Him which is able to
destroy both soul and body in hell...

She was travelling again...

Flying fast through the dark night sky, she arced left, then right and then against her will, that familiar pull drew her downward once more, to the earth.

Descending effortlessly, feet first, she heard the soft sound of gravel scrunch beneath her feet as she smoothly touched down.

In an unremarkable spot. No buildings, but here and there a leafless tree or two dotted the dark landscape, with ominous, spiny branches outstretched.

Looking around, she began walking forward with clusters of people. First three or four and then more, all walking in the same direction. Eventually their steps reduced to a crawl as they joined a slow-moving queue that curved off to the left to something she couldn't yet see, about a hundred paces ahead. She didn't join the line but instead walked on ahead in the darkness.

Curious, she stood a short distance away and from where she had a clear view of their destination, as the line disappeared into the entrance of a large cave. The pitch-blackness of the interior only lit up periodically, by a leaping red glow.

The sight should have been jarring enough, as realization of what she was witnessing dawned. Or perhaps the sound. The awful monotonous scraping of feet, endlessly shuffling along the graveled road, breaking the stillness of the night, and rattling her nerves.

But in truth, it was the smell that was most disturbing.

It filled her nostrils and enveloped her senses.

Burning sulfur…

She'd never smelt it before now, but instinctively she knew.

And unlike lambs to the slaughter, who would need to be led.

No.

Dear God…

They were all going in willingly.

No resistance, no fighting, no clawing hands as she'd imagined. No pleading cries rang out. Just that constant, agonizing, grating shuffle of dragging feet.

One by one, in single file, with heads bowed, they moved forward to be swallowed up by the great, yawning cavern. Each one clearly acknowledging they deserved this fate and that it was right, just, and inevitable that they had made…and should therefore have, their choice.

Separation…from God.

Having seen enough, she turned, ready to go back the way she'd come when she noticed him there. Standing at a distance just as she had been, his expression unreadable.

Oh, she knew who it was, intuitively, although this form was different. Morbidly curious she approached.

This time his hair was long and pitch black. He was monstrously tall, towering over her and solidly built. Arms crossed over his massive, bare chest; he looked down at her. His entire body pulsed with a reddish hue that swirled around and around, right beneath the surface of his skin, as though mere proximity to the cavern was making him burn, from the inside out.

Here was the very reason for those poor people's plight.

Her thoughts alive with curiosity, on pure impulse, she reached out to touch his impressive bicep. Felt the intense burning heat beneath her fingertip.

"OooWeee!!...ssss..." she made a hissing sound of steam with her tongue. "Yeah, that's *hot*!" She heard the words this time, sounding hollow and far away, as they echoed around her head. "Just look at you, standing way over here. You're not in charge of any of this. In fact, you're just like the rest of them. Just waiting for your turn."

Ordinarily she'd be readying herself, gathering a burst of power that would propel her at cheek-rippling speed, back into the dark skies, to flee. To hopefully jolt herself enough to wake from her nightmare. But no. Not this time. A slow-blossoming, faith-filled, prayer-based strength that had long since taken root, swelled up inside, bringing her back to her blessed, joy-filled best.

"Yep. Better get used to that heat there, buddy, cause...you and I both know that any day now...that's gonna be *ALL* you." She made a circling gesture with a hand to encompass the opening of the cavern, even as she felt laughter bubbling up. Irrational she knew, given what she'd just witnessed, but somehow perfectly apt when instinctively she knew she'd pissed him off with her little reminder about his well-deserved punishment.

Waking up to her lingering laughter, Rissa

grinned. Feeling much better than she had in weeks, she rose, eager to get ready for the day ahead and her planned night out.

Chapter 15

Romans 8:28

And we know that all things work together for good to them that love God, to them who are the called according to His purpose…

Yes. Scheduling time for a well-deserved night with friends was way overdue Rissa thought while she was getting ready for work in the morning. Dinner at one of those trendy new restaurants she'd heard so much about and some good conversation was just what the doctor ordered.

She grabbed an outfit to change into later and looked for her favorite shade of lipstick to complement it. When she didn't find it in her make-up drawer, she remembered she'd popped it into the evening bag she used the night of the Awards. She found it, along with an eyeliner pencil she thought she'd lost…and something else.

"What is that?" She reached in. Almost completely hidden in a corner of the lining was a tiny plastic case with a data dot. Wondering if it had come loose from the interactive show ticket which was also still in her bag, she dropped it into a pocket of her work handbag, so she could look at its contents at work, grabbed her car keys and headed out the door.

She went right to work as soon as she arrived, so it wasn't until she took a coffee break around 10am that she remembered the dot and tried to view it on her system. She tried a couple different things, but just couldn't get it open. With a wave of her hand, she brought up a listing of staff contacts on her screen and tapped the one for the IT manager.

"Hey Todd. How's it going?"

"I'm good Rissa." His life-sized smiling 3-D image - head to shoulders appeared, replacing her screen. "How about you?"

"Just trying to get the budgets done for the new campaign. Don't forget you need to give me some estimates for the associated system enhancements for Terri's new customer appreciation event."

"Oh yeah, definitely. I'm hoping to get those to you by end of week."

"Okay, great. Appreciate that. By the way, I

came across some tech from the Awards show and I was hoping you could lend me your expertise and help open it? I've tried everything I can think of and nothing worked." She twisted the small case around in her fingers and held it up for him to see.

"Okay." He leaned in for a closer look. "Well, I'm kinda swamped this week, what with your budgets and all." He grinned.

"Yeah, yeah," she laughed.

"But I'll tell you what, I'll come by your office after work and see what I can make of it, if you can hang around for a bit."

"Well, I've got dinner plans, but I guess I can push them if I need to. Thanks a lot Todd."

"Sure. I'll see you later." He rang off.

She put the dot in her desk drawer and went back to work.

Around 6.30pm, she changed for her dinner engagement, called her friends to let them know she might be late and then waited for Todd to arrive and work his magic.

"Sorry I'm so late." He hustled into her office nearly an hour later after a quick knock on her door jamb.

"No worries. Thanks again for doing me this favor." She retrieved the dot from her desk and handed it to him.

"May I?" he pointed to her screen.

"Yeah, of course." She relinquished her seat.

"Wow, you look great!" He eyed her from head to toe.

"Thanks." She smiled and tucked a few tendrils of hair behind her ear.

"Ok, so let's see what we've got here."

He sat, replaced her credentials with his and set to work. He expanded the dot and typed in something that revealed its inner coding. He tried a few things that didn't appear to work and then said, "Ok, I see what's happening here. I just need to write an algorithm to bypass these arrays–" his hands flew across the virtual keys for a few minutes, "–and add in a few loops." Another few minutes. "And…that's it."

"So, you realize, of course, I have absolutely no clue what you just said, or did, right?" She grinned and he shook his head on a laugh.

"That's okay. The main thing is you should be able to see what's on here now." He brought her credentials back up and left the dot on the screen.

"Just expand it and you're good to go." He looked at his watch. "I've gotta run. Have fun!" He jumped up and headed for the door. "Don't stay here too late and please be careful. I didn't see anyone else on the floor as I came in."

"Okay, I will. Have a great night and thanks again."

"Sure, you too," he said, as he disappeared through the doorway.

She retook her seat, put in her password, and touched the dot. It opened and she saw a palm of a hand that appeared to be fixing the view of whatever was behind, so it shifted a bit from left to right. The date stamp in the corner showed it was recorded the day before the Awards show. Then someone came into view.

"Oh my gosh…Margot?"

Oddly disturbing, it was like looking directly into her eyes as she peered right out of the screen. Then she moved back and quickly exited the room that came into frame. So, it was Margot who must have slipped the dot into her evening bag at the awards, likely when they were at the game table. But why?

"Wait, is that Dan's office?" Rissa recognized the huge potted plant he kept in a corner. Margot finally put a camera in his office. She'd said she wanted to catch him in the act when he was sexually harassing one of the women in the office so she could take the evidence to HR. Judging by the angle it must have been on his bookshelf.

Nothing happened as she watched for a couple minutes, so she used the motion circle to forward the footage. The images accelerated and she saw Dan zip in and out, along with a couple other people. She speeded up again until he was just sitting at his desk.

"Probably playing video games, or watching porn," she snorted and forwarded again, racing past shots of just the empty room, and then stopped as she spotted something. She rewound a few frames to time stamp 7.42pm.

He came into the office, with someone.

"Who is that?" Rissa spread her forefinger and thumb to zoom in. She didn't recognize the woman who was nicely dressed, slim, with blond hair. Dan went over to his desk while she stayed at the door looking around and smiling. Regretting she couldn't hear their conversation, or read lips, Rissa watched as he grabbed a lovely, wrapped gift box from one of his desk drawers and handed it to the woman. She beamed, said something and then he ushered her out the door. Not more than a minute later he came back in and there was a bright flash of light all around him that made her screen go black for a moment.

"What in the world?" Rissa leaned in to get a better look as the picture returned.

It was no longer Dan who stood in frame. The person's back was facing the camera, but she could see that it was a very tall, muscled and blond-haired man. "Oh crap…is that the GQ-holo guy?" She zoomed in as far as she could as he stood unmoving for a long moment and then another.

But then in the very next minute, she was looking at Dan again, as he turned and exited the room.

She rewound and looked at it again, twice, hoping to get a better look at his face, and to see if she'd missed anything. She really couldn't tell if he was the one from the awards show, but quite obviously it had to be one of those defender demons, right? But...

"Of course!" She spoke out loud again, as light dawned. "Margot... She must have thought she'd stumbled onto the story of the century – a defender who could shape shift and transform into Dan."

Knock. Knock.

She jumped and looked up from the screen towards her door. Icy dread gripped her. It was Dan. He was standing in her doorway.

"You really should stop that you know."

"Dan?"

"I said..."

"Stop. Calling me that."

The words were a rich and deeply masculine rumble, albeit clipped and cold as ice.

Definitely not Dan...

He stepped into her office and turned. Took his time reaching for the sensor and in watching the door slowly close, with a soft whistle.

Terrified, she realized this was not just some random alien demon, this was the serial killer–the very peril her guardian had warned her against was here. "Al? You there?" she whispered. When he didn't answer or appear, as discreetly as she could she touched the speed dial on her watch.

"This is Detective Duncan Wright. Kindly leave

a message."

"Detective, I think I'm in danger–" she whispered, just as her visitor pierced her with a glare and began to approach. "–I'm at my office, please…hurry."

Thinking to make a run past him for the door, she jumped out of her chair and made it around the front of her desk and then froze in place, nearly blinded, as he halted in the middle of the room.

Blinding light bursting from every orifice of his body, he began to change…

Chapter 16

Romans 3:23-24
For all have sinned, and come short of the glory of God;
Being justified freely by His grace through the
redemption that is in Christ Jesus…

Transformed. Into a creature of light and deep darkness.

Forced to shield her eyes from the harsh brightness of the change process, between her fingers Rissa caught short glimpses as Dan's features and body type contorted and twisted, lengthened, and re-formed into a tall, well-built and strikingly handsome being.

"Dear God, have mercy." She lowered her hands and made two important discoveries.

It wasn't the GQ-holo guy, and Dan…was dead.

In that very instant she acknowledged what this all meant. The unremarkable little weatherman was gone. Killed. Who knew how many weeks earlier. Never coming back. She'd be the first to say he was annoying as all hell, and they'd certainly had their differences. Professional and personal. But an immediate wave of deep and very genuine distress enveloped her. Tears sprang to her eyes even as a word of prayer for his soul and for help for herself bubbled up in her heart and mind.

Back to the matter at hand, she sniffed as she blinked her tears away and immediately brought 'him' back into focus.

Wow, he's bewitching.

The words just popped into her head. Very accurate and so very alarming. Hands down he was easily the best-looking person she'd ever seen in her life.

He looked like a man…but at the same time, didn't.

His features—too well-proportioned, too perfect, were the very picture of ordered symmetry. His actions too fluid—the economy and careful precision of his every movement fairly screamed of barely leashed power. And as if that weren't enough, the glowing red aura that surrounded and seemed to emanate from him in pulses was otherworldly and unlike anything she'd seen outside of her night travels.

Yes, God's angels were certainly a wonder to behold.

Her thoughts flew to Alcindor. Her protector was the truest of servants of the Most High.

Surely then he must be even more…

An unimaginable beauty, to be sure…

Same as those on the wrong side of eternity it seemed.

Brought sharply back to the present by the sight of his menacing form, she marveled that a monumental fall from grace and millennia trapped on earth had failed to dim such beauty–present circumstances aside, the very splendor of God's creation had a whole new meaning for her now.

All except for his eyes though. There was something about them. Sharply intelligent and icy-grey malevolence. So alive, yet so cold–glinting with what she could only describe as pure evil.

And death.

She began to back away, still stunned by his extraordinarily magnificent, malignant beauty. And then she heard his voice, his real voice, for the second time that night.

"And now you know."

There it was again. That rich, deep rumble, appealing to something deep inside her, completely against her will.

At least five different questions flashed through

her mind, each one fighting for prominence, even as she thought of how best to distract him and buy herself some more time till help came… she hoped.

Exactly how long had it taken for Al to show up when she'd needed aid in the past? Now she really wished she'd paid more attention. She continued inching back as he advanced on her, matching her step for step. He didn't even pause when he came into line with her desk and waved a casual hand over the data file.

"Thank you, Rissy. I've been looking for that."

She winced at an explosion that jarred her senses and shattered the damning data dot into dust. Her back hit the wall and with that came the fresh realization there was nowhere left to run. He was now so close she felt his breath on her face as he peered down at her.

"Why…ah…ahem," she cleared her throat, mentally shook herself and settled on one of her questions.

Flattery…

"Of all the people you could have picked, why Dan? I mean…just look at you… Wow."

"Easy."

His smile weakened her knees… just the tiniest bit.

"He was the perfect disguise. I mean…just look at me," he parroted her words, replicating her voice exactly she noted with some alarm.

He took a step or two away from her and casually gestured with a hand down the gorgeous, lean, and muscled length of his body. "I would have drawn far too much attention to myself like this."

He said it with such breathtaking, sickening arrogance she didn't know if she wanted to swoon, or vomit. Instead, she took a tiny breath and felt a sense of relief in that moment that he'd put a small distance between them with his action. But then very nearly jumped out of her skin in the next, when without warning–

"*You* just do not know!" he barked. "Not one of you, could *ever* understand what it was like! Watching the first of you…created lower. Inferior. Yet still so loved. The precious. Crowned with glory and honor." He snarled, then paced further away and then back towards her again as he ran agitated fingers through the thick waves of his golden hair.

"When I…when *we*… first got here, eons ago. We had to start a whole new existence. We were so afraid at first, realizing we had made the wrong choice." His eyes darted around for a moment as he rubbed his brow. "We lived in constant fear of His return and that ultimate and inevitable destruction." He gave a short laugh. If you could call such a hollow sound one of humor.

Al's dire reference and a memory of a pertinent line from a bible verse whispered through her worried mind.

We…are…Legion.

Were there more of them in the room, even now? She pushed the speculation out and fought to focus just on him and what he was saying.

"But then time wore on and on…we existed only to do Lucifer's bidding and as we learned everything about you humans, bent minds, and turned more and more souls…*I* began to realize I could use that knowledge to do so much more. After all, why stop at leading a man to damnation, when you could just as easily kill one as well."

He nodded at her, as though she should share his understanding of the connection between the two thoughts.

"At first it was just for sport and just the ones I knew were irredeemable. I'd work my way into their dreams then eventually, when the time was right, into their lives. I even gave myself a name, an identity," he grated. "Oh, I set myself apart all right.

"And then one night, a long time ago, I had occasion to release the soul of a particular young female. Oh, I'd been trying to corrupt her for years. But she just wouldn't turn. A soul so pure, you could see her light for miles." He sounded wistful as a strange look flashed across his face.

"A rare one she was indeed. I got so angry one night instead of just messing with her dreams, I woke her up. Sat right beside her in bed. Just wanted to frighten her, at first. But then she looked right at me.

No fear. 'So, it's finally come to this,' she said, so calm and so resolute. Like she knew exactly what was going to happen, even before I did. I was so angry. I brought all my power to bear, concentrated it around her neck." He gestured with menacing hands as though he were in the moment. "Right over that necklace with the little gold cross that was her prized possession, and I choked every bit of life, right out of her.

"I felt it then, for just a few precious moments as she made the great change. The most intoxicating, most exquisite sensation I've experienced in eons. The joy of the redeemed. Her soul and spirit rejoicing as she entered bliss, was like nothing I'd ever known. So potent, so enveloping. So much greater than my own joy had ever been." His voice softened and he looked pensive, yet envious all at the same time.

"After that I just couldn't get enough. It became like I imagine an addiction is for you humans," he sneered, as though the association with mankind's weakness disgusted him. Then he pierced her with his fierce glare.

"And years have come and gone since then, Alrissa," he began to walk back towards her, "so…as you're about to discover, I've become particularly proficient at ushering you humans from this world, on into the next."

Frantic, she looked about her, still trying to think of how she might evade him until either Al or the

Detective, or anybody really, could arrive to save her.

"Oh, he won't save you this time."

"What?" Her gaze snapped back to his.

"Your angel. You know him, don't you?" His eyes flashed with even more deep-seated anger and hatred.

"I'm curious," she evaded his question and asked another of her own. "How did you even know about Margot?"

"One of *them* saw her the night she collected that little bit of theatre she recorded, and informed me."

"And Dan? Ah…I mean, how did you even meet him? Surely, he wasn't a pure soul?"

"Oh no," he barked out a laugh. "Far from it. You have absolutely no idea how vile and depraved his thoughts of you were, little one."

His disgusting, lustful look…made her super uncomfortable.

"Hell… I even inspired some of them myself."

His words–made her feel even worse.

With a gesture he indicated her office. "One night I saw your pathetic little would-be suitor coming out of here, followed him out onto the street. Watched him, try to break into the conversation of some of your colleagues who were standing on the corner. They didn't even spare him a second glance. It looked like they could care less what he had to say. And as I've learned over time, just become another insignificant, Godless weasel and not one of you would even notice me." His words dripped venom from gritted teeth. "They never even look twice. Everyone just dismisses me. I become… invisible."

He looked down at his feet.

"I suppose I could have just possessed him, but then I–"

"But then you blamed him too–"

His gaze snapped back up to hers.

"–for putting you in a position to need, to crave, his anonymity. The same way you blame us all for our reaction to these 'inferior' personas you adopt?" She whispered the question almost to herself, in disbelief.

He looked confused, or perhaps it was surprise at her insight that flittered across his flawless face for a moment before he nodded slowly.

"So, you killed him instead." A statement more than a question. "Just like you killed them all. All those people?!"

Suddenly she was angry.

"They weren't responsible. They did nothing to invite this. Say what you like, but this has nothing to do with you stealing souls, or reclaiming your bliss. Maybe that's how it started, but this is all about you now. Because what? You want to be 'seen' now?! You choose to become some less than attractive person and then despise the world for reacting to you exactly as you intended?! How could you do that?!"

Suddenly she looked past the impossibly special and uniquely beautiful façade and saw the singular evil beneath. He was just like every self-absorbed, hate-filled narcissist she'd ever met. To her, he could have been a flawed human in that moment and just like that she lost her fear and remembered who she was–a precious, beloved child of the King, and it was high time she acted like it.

Her weapons were not of this earth. They were not carnal. They were of Almighty God for the pulling down of evil strong holds, just like this. Closing her eyes, she quieted her mind and focused with her spirit. She took a deep breath–

Surrender…and believe.

–And released it. Felt it swirl all around her, fill with power and light every fiber of her being. Her entire body vibrated, as she gave herself completely over to God's will.

In the spirit, she saw him–arms outstretched as his red aura was hit over and over with a series of pure, white-hot energy bursts that emanated from all around her. They pummeled him till he was thrown back and away from her like a ragdoll. Until he could no longer stand.

He slumped against her then and her eyes snapped open as automatically she grasped him to herself and fell with a small cry, as she bore the full weight of his big body down to the floor. She ended up pinned beneath him, breathing in short, deep gasps. Her shoulder painfully pressed against the wall, her legs at an awkward angle beneath her, his head cradled on her lap.

"What?" Her gaze snapped down to his as he whispered and breathed words that sounded like relief to her.

Although…he seemed to be looking right past her…

The Son of Man walked towards him. His pace—unhurried, smooth, and steady. Much like the man. Regal. Wreathed in an aura of quiet strength and eternal power. He stopped a few paces away, evoking real fear.

Choking, life-ending fear, stronger than any emotion he'd ever experienced in his very long existence.

And acceptance.

No running this time. He deserved this end.

He'd done so much wrong for so long. Wielded what he'd thought was power over life and death. But not really. Not ever.

Here was the One in Three. Imbued with the power to destroy both body and soul.

Yes. Here was real power.

And truth.

And light.

So much light…

With a slight smile, the One nodded, just once.

Ah…there it was…he remembered that feeling, from eons before. Had almost forgotten the sheer intensity of it. The very same that he'd been trying to reclaim each time he took a life–that strong, all-consuming, unfathomable peace and supreme joy now washed over and through him. The only difference was that now, it came with a new and truly miraculous truth for him and with a clear understanding.

That having separated himself from Legion, he could choose. It was just that simple.

Choose truth. Choose to repent, by His blessed grace and return to a life of unending joy, in the most excellent and most glorious of service. Or else be swallowed up and destroyed by the terrible, awful lie with which he allowed himself to be deceived so very long ago.

Even then it was lurking just at the very edge of his mind. Envy. Hatred. Darkness. Evil. An evil, every bit as prideful as its original and most ardent proponent. So familiar now, ever since he'd allowed it to creep in and join with his very being.

But not the anger though.

No.

That was all theirs.

He could still feel them. A multitude of hellishly enraged minions. Knowing just as he did, that they were forever destined to end. The battle long ago won - on that torturous wooden cross. Settled. Even from the very foundations of time.

He looked to the One and knew. Choose the right path this time and forgiveness, or be lost. Lost and buried in an anguish of never-ending darkness and tormented separation.

Forever.

He'd never dared hope…but now…

"Finally… It's over."

He meant the words for them, but didn't even spare a look back, could care less about their writhing, seething, monstrous rage. Even so, they dared not approach, could not exist in the presence of the Son of Man, unless He willed it.

Decision made; he stood.

Took one step forward and then another…mirroring outstretched arms…he was lifted, to redemption.

———•◼•———

"What?" Rissa repeated, trying to understand.

But it was too late. She watched spellbound as his very last breath escaped his lips.

"He's gone."

She jerked at the soft words and hit her head against the wall.

"Darn it, Al! You scared the life out of me.

Again!" She winced and rubbed the back of her head with one hand and then took his with the other, as he pulled her upright.

"Wait…where'd he go?" She looked about, trying to wrap her brain around the disappearance of the body she'd just cradled in her lap.

In the blink of an eye…

"Like I said, he's gone. He won't bother you or anyone else, ever again."

"Yeah and no thanks to you Guardian."

He grinned. "Come on, I was right here, watching the entire time and I happen to know you just took your faith journey to a-whole-nother level, so I'd call that a win." He held up a palm, she assumed for her to air high-five.

She frowned at him instead.

"No? Gonna leave me hanging huh. Okay then."

"Uh, yeah. I'm still mad at you. I was terrified! And when you didn't show, I didn't know what to think. I mean, oh my gosh…did you see that guy?!" She slapped a hand to her forehead.

"He was really gorgeous though, wasn't he…?" She moved the hand to her throat as her thoughts did a full three-hundred-and-sixty-degree turn, taking her right back to her first impression. "So tall and built and just dripping sex-appeal. Which reminds me–"

Al's voice - dropped an octave. "Seriously?"

His expression - unreadable.

"Whaaat?"

"Mega filter-failure Rissa…of like *epic* proportion–" he indicated the magnitude with outstretched hands, "–even for you."

"No. It's not what you think–" she raced to make her point, "–it's just that seeing him made me wonder…about you I mean…and…what you look like. So, is that really you? Or…" she crossed her arms over her chest to lock in nervous energy and rocked back on a heel.

He gave a slow negative shake of his head in response, even as the left corner of his mouth quirked upward.

"Okay. Really?" She cleared her throat as her voice cracked.

"Interesting, interesting," she continued in a musical tone, "I figured as much, so…if you *are* anything like that too–" she moved her hands around and flexed to signify a tall, hunky guy, "–I was thinking that in the circumstances, the least you could do is…yuh know–?" she bobbed her head from left to right, "–let me just take a quick peak? I mean, couldn't you just–?"

"To what end Alrissa Catherine Cole?"

"And there you go again, with my full name and the crisp English, and answering a question with a question." She raised her hands and then dropped them. They made a slapping sound as they hit the front of her thighs on their return. "I feel like I'm in private school again, facing my Head Mistress for heaven's sake. Oh, never mind," she sighed as he grinned. "I already know what it means when you do that."

"Look," he sobered, "I feel like I should explain, this was always going to be about you learning to truly let go and let God. The human journey of faith is *all* about learning to look only to Him. For He alone is The All Powerful One, Creator, Comforter, Provider, Deliverer, Healer, Protector. He alone is your source for all things great, and small.

"It's about relationship, trusting and surrendering. Over and over again. And in your human frailty it's about knowing that even on your worst days, when you get it completely wrong. He is sufficient.

"In a word – it's about love. His love. Unselfish, enduring, unconditional, all-encompassing love.

"I've seen countless humans leave this earth, Rissa. The ones who accept Him as Savior and the ones who do not. And of all the ones who accept that most precious gift of salvation, at the very moment of transition they talk to me not of possessions, or even regret, they speak only of love."

She was awed and deeply moved by the life-altering significance of his words, but still felt uneasy in the wake of everything she'd been through.

"But what about the fallen? They're all still out there. What if–?"

"And they've always been out there. Sure, they've stepped out of the shadows, but seen or unseen, their modus operandi is the same as it's always been. Just keep faith child of God and all will be well."

She basked in the heartfelt reassurance in his eyes and even more in the gentle brush of his hand against her cheek and chin. Her heart skipped a beat, and she felt a familiar warmth blossom.

"And what about us?" she ventured, bolstered by the sincerity of his words. "Did you give any thought to that?"

Now or never…lay it all on the line girl…

"I feel like we have this special connection and I'll regret it for the rest of my life if I don't at least explore where it could go." She heard his deep inward breath and got even more lost in his loving gaze.

"Come on now…we talked about this, Rissa. You're *my* person, remember?" He caressed her cheek with the backs of gentle fingers. "I've been with you from the beginning, since you were a baby and but for these highly unusual circumstances, you'd never *ever*, have even known I was there.

"Is the connection you feel real? No doubt. And is there love? Absolutely."

"Well then–"

"But…it's not the kind of love you'd have for one of your own kind."

"But why?" She pursed her lips in what she hoped was a pretty pout. "I don't understand. Why couldn't we just try." She ran her hands down his arms and grasped his hands in hers. Absorbed and savored the pure and potent goodness and joy that was him. "You could choose, can't you? Choose to be with me." The minute the words were out she cringed at the note of pleading she'd allowed to creep into her voice.

"Choose you? Over the Alpha and Omega?" he asked in a soft tone. "Are you even listening to yourself?" He shook his head and gently broke their contact as he took a few steps away.

"I'm a messenger of God, Rissa. Forget the fact it's what I was made for. It's *the* single most amazing existence, you could never imagine!" His face shone, his smile so brilliant, she forgot her disappointment at his rejection and marveled at the obvious delight of his affirmation.

"Forget what you've seen in movies. No angel will ever choose to fall. Not ever again. Trust me. Even the prospect of separation fills me, fills us all, with unimaginable, spirit-destroying dread. I wish I could describe the Glory to you, or the joy and the awesome wonders of heaven–" he moved in close again, "–but you lack the ability to comprehend it, I'm afraid. It would probably melt your little brain." He laughed and she swatted his hand away as he tweaked her nose.

"Okay, okay. I had to try." She held up her hands in mock surrender.

"Rissa," he pulled her close and turned her chin in his direction. "I want you to know, I'm really glad you got through all of this. I can see just how difficult it's all been for you." He looked deep into her eyes. "You are absolutely amazing, and I'd do anything for you, I mean, to keep you safe. You know that? Right?"

She nodded.

"So, question for real this time. Now that the danger is passed–" she drew in a stuttered breath, "–will I ever see you again?"

He smiled and as he leaned towards her, she closed her eyes, held her breath, and for the first time, felt the gentle touch of his cheek brush hers and an even softer whisper echoing at her ear.

"Pray…"

She opened her eyes and sighed.

Utterly alone, she turned. Caught sight of her solitary reflection, looking right back, surrounded by the vast night sky… beyond her unyielding and isolating glass wall.

Chapter 17

Revelation 21:5
And He that sat upon the throne said Behold, I make all things new…

"Alrissa! You in there?!" Detective Wright burst through the door before it slid fully open. Rissa spun in the direction of his voice, startled for yet another time that night.

"Oh, thank God." He got to her in three quick strides. "I got your message. Are you okay?" His gaze covered her from head to toe, then he pulled her into a close embrace at her nod. "You sounded terrified on the phone. What's happened?"

"Nothing really, I'm actually fine." Mild surprise at their first such intimate contact aside, she melted into the cocoon created by his chest and arms and drew on his strength. Raw and real, she absorbed this new-found comfort.

Mmm...

"Oh wow...you smell *so-oo* good, for a cop," she blurted out before she could stop herself.

100% masculine and like lemony, woodsy luxury.

How had she not noticed that before now?

"Thank you?" He pulled away a bit and gave her a quizzical look. "And how exactly, in your estimation, *should* a cop smell, Miz Cole?" An attractive half smile played on his lips as they separated.

She barked out a laugh. "Well not like you, that's for sure. And touché, Detective." She wagged a finger at him. "Good one. You got me."

"Not yet...but here's hoping."

Woah...

She tucked the strands of hair that had come loose from her bun behind her ear and then tugged on the ends of her patterned blazer to smooth out the wrinkles from her prior exertions.

She looked further down. At her favorite heels, at a coffee stain on the carpet. Anywhere, except at him, as she felt a blast of unprecedented heat flood her, at his softly spoken words.

She looked up. Met his gaze and lost her breath...as she slammed right into inescapable, deep blue mastery, all wrapped up in…Enveloping. Intriguing. Declared. Resolve.

"Uh…so anyway," she tried to gather her thoughts. "Thanks so much for coming to check on me. I-uh thought someone was following me earlier, and I got a bit freaked out, but it turned out to be nothing really." She gestured around the empty room. "Sorry for wasting your time," she ventured a sheepish apology, uncomfortable about breaking her rule with the lie. But she couldn't very well tell him she and her Guardian Angel just presided over the demise of a killer who was also an alien-demon, could she?

"No need to apologize. I was just about to call you when I got your voice message. We got the guy. Killed himself tragically. Found evidence and a confession at his home for all the murders and even an attempt on your life that day I saved you, outside the church. So, case closed."

"Wow…Really?" She took a moment to let the news sink in and didn't let on that she also knew the church incident wasn't an accident. "Who was it?"

"An unregistered defender. He wasn't even in the system, so no priors. Apparently, he was some kind of outcast. An aberration, with special powers. Craziest thing I've ever seen in all my years on the force, plus, something tells me this may just be the beginning of a much larger issue involving Verndari." He shook his head and rubbed a hand over his long past five PM shadow.

"Yeah. I'll bet," she said partly to herself, aware that he didn't yet know the half of it.

So, Mr. Drop-Dead-Gorgeous demon/alien had covered his tracks.

She'd have to ponder that little bit of news later.

"So… now, that the case involving you is over–" he reached out, pulled her close and cupped her chin for a moment, to turn her face up to his, "–I want you to know, I'm really glad you got through all of this. I can see just how difficult it's all been for you." Her breath caught at the familiar words so recently uttered and at the sincerity in the eyes of the one who now spoke them.

"You are absolutely amazing, and I'd do anything for you, I mean, to keep you safe–

"–You know that? Right?"

Really Al? Word for word huh…

She looked down at her shoes again, this time to hide her grin, because she just *knew* somewhere in glorious heaven, Al was laughing his adorable head off.

"Yeah…I think I do, now." She lifted her gaze to his and then lost her breath again, as he raised her left hand and without breaking eye contact, pressed his perfect lips to her knuckles in a soft and sensual kiss.

"I thought you said you weren't a gentleman, Detective." Her voice was a near whisper.

"I'm not," he growled, as he bent, grasped the back of her head, captured her lips, and devoured her mouth…by slow, hot, and sweet degrees.

Holy cow! Who IS this guy?

"By the way–" he pulled back a fraction, his voice a gravelly rumble that started a vibration in her toes, that climbed to other regions, "–my name…" he kissed her again, deep and soft, "…is Duncan."

Smiling, he lowered her hand that he'd never let go of and clasped it in both of his.

In a warm grasp.

That felt like forever.

"Are you hungry? Can I interest you in some dinner?"

"Yeah, uh…I could eat," she managed. Still a bit lightheaded from the most amazing kisses of her life, she grabbed her handbag and let him lead her from the room.

"Great! Do you like cheesecake? I know this place that serves *the* most amazing chocolate cheesecake…"

She listened as he began to describe some of the restaurant's other delicacies, even as in her heart, she raised a prayer to heaven in thanksgiving for all new and unexpected blessings.

—•●•—

"So, all things considered, we could–" Alcindor

held up a finger, "–Hang on…"

He roared with laughter and slapped Michael on the back, as though the Archangel knew the reason for his amusement.

"Oh, it's Rissa," he said as he noticed the look of confusion on his friend's face. He paused again and then smiled "I think she's going to be just fine."

"Glad to hear it. I still can't believe how she moved so many to sing along with her, in the presence of such evil. It is truly remarkable. And such a blessing to me. What a privilege, to be chosen to rescue her at that pivotal moment in her life. Got a bit sticky for her for a while there?"

"Never. Her faith is strong. She's a true believer."

"Good. I like her," he gave a slight smile.

"Well, I better get back before I'm missed. I know who their next target is, so I'll start running interference. Remember what we discussed Alcindor, I need someone in law enforcement who I can depend on to go where I may not. We'll talk more, next time we meet?" In an instant he transformed, his abundant light and perfect visage hidden, as he assumed the form of the one Legion called…Svikari.

"Definitely. Leave it to me. The Redeemer is seeking just the person."

———— •●• ————

At the very speed of thought, Alcindor transcended both space and time and stood at the door of the 15th precinct of the local PD. It slid open and he walked slowly to the desk.

"Good morning," he greeted the sitting Sergeant.

"Here, let me help you old-timer." The Sergeant pushed a button on his desk. The shimmering energy field surrounding his unit glided down from the ceiling and disappeared into the floor, then slid back up again as soon he exited. He ushered Alcindor to a seat in the nearby visitors' chairs.

"Thank you, young man. God bless you." He set his cane to the side and took the seat indicated.

"What can we do for you today?" The Seargent smiled at him.

"It's a matter of some concern and I've heard there's a detective here I can speak to about it."

"Sure. What's his name?"

"*Her* name actually…Almonzo."

EPILOGUE

That night Rissa gave vent to all her pent-up feelings as she let cleansing tears flow for the first time in years.

She cried over the losses of the past and in the joy of new beginnings.

She cried and prayed for herself, for her family and friends, for Dan, for Helen, for Margot and especially for the families of all the dead. And oddly enough, even for him.

In the moment she'd sat with his head cradled in her lap, and despite knowing what he was, she dared hope he'd found some semblance of peace at the end.

It was in his last whispered word really.

Just the one… for it was pure power…

"Jesus."

Love is Deborah Lamoreaux's raison d'être.

She lives to immerse her readers in a rich fantasy world where magical faraway places and unwavering fated love all come together to create a delicious, satisfying melting pot of literary distraction.

In her world love is always true, unexpected, undeniable, unconditional and of course… everlasting.

Ms. Lamoreaux only ever comes alive when she's let loose to produce her next work of romantic fiction and each and every time that you journey alongside her, within the pages of one of her creations, she escapes the confines of imagination…
So come, escape with her…